'...ce?   think it has the
power ... _ . .   .u.

'You've been playing with n...

'Couldn't resist it. There – one mag... e or blanks, and one spare. Use your initiative, James. Good luck.' He looked at his watch. 'You have three minutes.'

Bond quickly reconnoitred the building and placed himself in the upper corridor, since it had no windows. He stayed close to the door which opened on to the landing, but was well shielded by the corridor wall. He was crouched against the wall when the stun grenades exploded in the hallway below – two ear-splitting crumps, followed by several bursts of automatic fire. Bullets hacked and chipped into the plaster and brickwork on the other side of the wall, while another burst almost took the door beside him off its hinges.

They were not using blanks. This was for real, and he knew with sudden shock, that it was as he had earlier deduced. He was being thrown to the wolves.

John Gardner served with the Fleet Air Arm and Royal Marines before embarking on a long career as a thriller writer, including international bestsellers *The Nostradamus Traitor*, *The Garden of Weapons*, *Confessor* and *Maestro*. In 1981 he was invited by Glidrose Publications Ltd – now known as Ian Fleming Publications – to revive James Bond in a brand new series of novels. To find out more visit John Gardner's website at www.john-gardner.com or the Ian Fleming website at www.ianfleming.com

ROLE OF HONOUR

John Gardner

For
Beryl and Gil

An Orion paperback

First published in Great Britain in 1984
by Jonathan Cape
This paperback edition published in 2012
by Orion Books Ltd,
Orion House, 5 Upper St Martin's Lane,
London WC2H 9EA

An Hachette UK company

1 3 5 7 9 10 8 6 4 2

A CIP catalogue record for this book
is available from the British Library.

ISBN 978-1-4091-3565-4

Typeset at The Spartan Press Ltd,
Lymington, Hants

Printed and bound by CPI Group (UK) Ltd,
Croydon, CR0 4YY

The Orion Publishing Group's policy is to use papers
that are natural, renewable and recyclable products and
made from wood grown in sustainable forests. The logging
and manufacturing processes are expected to conform to
environmental regulations of the country of origin.

www.orionbooks.co.uk
www.ianfleming.com

CONTENTS

I

ROBBERY WITH VIOLETS

The robbery of security vans can take place at any time of the day, though, as a rule, the Metropolitan Police do not encounter hijackers attempting a quick getaway during the rush hour. Neither do they expect trouble with a cargo that is sewn up tight. Only a privileged few knew exactly when the Kruxator Collection would arrive in the country. That it was due to come to Britain was common knowledge, and you had only to read a newspaper to discover that March 15th was the day on which the tabled group of paintings and jewellery were to go on display – for two weeks – at the Victoria and Albert Museum.

The Kruxator Collection is called after its founder, the late Niko Kruxator, whose fabulous wealth arose from sources unknown, for he had arrived penniless in the United States at about the time of the Wall Street Crash in October 1929. By the time he died in 1977, most people thought of him as the Greek shipping magnate, but he still held his interest in Kruxator Restaurants, and the great international chain of Krux-Lux Hotels. He was also sole owner of the Kruxator Collection, which he left to the country of his adoption – all 300 paintings and 700 fantastic *objets d'art*, including three icons dating back to the fifteenth century, smuggled out of Russia at the time of the Revolution, and no less than sixteen pieces once owned by the Borgias: a collection beyond price, though insured for billions of dollars.

The two-week London showing of the Kruxator Collection

would be the last in its tour of European capitals before the whole consignment was returned to New York. Niko had been shrewd enough to leave an endowment for a gallery in which these priceless objects could be displayed. He wanted to be remembered, and had taken steps to make certain that his name would be linked with those of Van Gogh, Breughel, El Greco, Matisse, Picasso and others. Not that he was knowledgeable about art, but he could sense a fair bargain which would appreciate in value, and had acquired the collection as an investment.

A private security firm looked after the precious paintings, drawings and gems on a permanent basis, though host countries were expected to provide extra cover. Nobody was in any doubt that the two armoured vans that carried the exhibits were at constant risk. When the collection was on display, an elaborate system of electronics protected every item.

The cargo came into Heathrow on an unannounced 747 at six minutes past four in the afternoon. The Boeing was directed to an unloading bay far away from the passenger terminals – near the old Hunting Clan hangars, which still display the name of that company in large white letters.

The armoured vans were waiting. They had arrived by the sea route after depositing the collection the previous evening at the Charles De Gaulle airport in Paris. Two unmarked police cars, each containing four armed plainclothes officers, were now in attendance.

The loaders were trusted employees of the Kruxator Agency who knew their task so well that the entire cargo was off the aircraft and packed into the vans in less than an hour. The unremarkable convoy, led by one of the police cars, the other taking up the rear, set off to make a circuit of the perimeter before joining the normal flow of traffic through the underpass and out on to the M4 motorway. It was just after five-fifteen and the light was beginning to go, with traffic starting to build up both in and out of the capital. Even so, within half an hour the procession would arrive at the end of the motorway where the road narrows to two lanes, taking vehicles on to what is dubiously known as the Hammersmith Flyover, and then into the Cromwell Road.

Later reports from the police cars – which were in touch by radio with the armoured vans – showed a certain amout of confusion during the early part of the journey. An eye-catching black girl, driving a violet-coloured sports car, managed to come between the leading car and the first van just as the convoy climbed the ramp on to the Flyover; while an equally striking white girl, in a violet dress, driving a black sports car, cut in between the second van and the police car in the rear.

At first nothing alarming was reported over the radios, though the police vehicles and the armoured vans were being separated even further by the manoeuvres of the two girls who had tucked the violet Lancia and the black Ferrari neatly into the convoy. The trailing police car made two efforts to overtake and get back into position but was thwarted by the Ferrari. Each time it either swung out to prevent the police car from getting in, or pulled over to allow other vehicles to overtake. The Lancia was carving up the front part of the convoy in a similar way. By the time they reached the Cromwell Road not only had the gap widened between the police cars and the armoured vans, but the two vans had also been parted.

The route had been chosen to ensure maximum security. The convoy was to swing left off the Cromwell Road and proceed into Kensington High Street, then turn right before Knightsbridge, reaching Exhibition Road via the one-way system so as to gain access to the rear of the Victoria and Albert Museum, well away from the exposed main entrance.

One police car had reached the Royal Garden Hotel, on the High Street side of Kensington Gardens, and the other was only just entering the far end of the High Street, when radio communications ceased.

The car in front broke all security regulations, activating its

Klaxon and U-turning across a blocked mass of traffic to make its way back along Kensington High Street. The rear car, also in some panic, began to move aggressively. A chaos of honking, hooting vehicles was suddenly smothered in a thick pall of choking, violet-coloured smoke. Later, the drivers and shotgun riders of the two vans gave identical accounts of what happened: 'The coloured smoke was just there. No warning, no bombs, nothing, just dense, purple smoke out of nowhere. Then everything in the cab went live, as though we'd developed some terrible electrical fault. When that happens you turn off the engine, but the shocks kept coming, and we knew we could be electrocuted. Getting out was a gut reaction . . .'

No one remembered anything after escaping from the vans, and all four men were later discovered, still in safety helmets and flak jackets, neatly laid out on the pavement. They were treated for respiratory problems, as were many others who had been in the vicinity, for the smoke had an unpleasant effect on the lungs.

The two vans simply disappeared, as though a hole had opened up in the road, engulfed them, and then closed over again.

The police officer in charge of the investigation appeared on News at Ten that evening saying that the robbery had been planned to the second. It must have been rehearsed again and again. In fact, as he confided to his colleagues beforehand, so precise was the timing that you might well suppose it to have been a computerised theft. The only clues were the two sports cars and the descriptions of their drivers. The Central Registry, however, soon revealed that the sports cars' number plates – noted accurately by police officers – had never been issued to any vehicle.

The Kruxator robbery was daring, exact, brilliant and very costly. The lack of progress made by the police investigating it remained in the headlines for the best part of a month. Even the sly comments suggesting a breach of security, and the sudden resignation of a senior member of the Secret Intelligence Service – by name, Commander James Bond – were relegated to a corner of page two and soon lost altogether to the public eye.

2

OUTER DARKNESS

In the beginning, Standing Orders were quite clear. Paragraph 12(c) instructed that,

> *Any officer classified as being on active duty who is subject to any alteration in private financial status will inform Head of A Section giving full details and providing any documentation that is thought either necessary or desirable by him.*

Section A is, of course, Accounts, but confidential information – such as James Bond's Australian legacy – automatically went personally to M, Records, and the Chief-of-Staff as well.

In the ordinary commercial world, Bond would have received numerous warm expressions of congratulation on his unexpected windfall. Not so in the Service. Those who work for Records are tight-lipped by tradition as well as training. Neither M nor Bill Tanner would think of bringing the matter up, for both were of the old school which rightly considered details of private money to be of a personal nature. The fact that they both knew would never stop them pretending they did not. It was, then, almost a shock when M himself mentioned it.

The months immediately prior to Bond receiving the news of his legacy had been dull with routine. He always found the paperwork part of his job debilitating and boring, but that summer – now eighteen months ago – was particulary irksome, especially as he had taken all his leave early, a mistake which condemned him to day after day of files, memos, directives and other people's reports. As so often happened in Bond's world there was absolutely nothing – not even a simple confidential courier job – to alleviate the drudgery of those hot months.

Then, early in the following November, came the legacy. It arrived in a thick manila envelope with a Sydney postmark, falling literally out of the blue with a heavy plop through his letter box. The letter was from a firm of solicitors who for many years had acted for the younger brother of Bond's father, an uncle whom Bond had never seen. Uncle Bruce, it appeared, had died a wealthy man, leaving every penny of his estate to his nephew James, who hitherto had enjoyed little private money. Now his fortunes were drastically changed.

The whole settlement came to around a quarter of a million sterling. There was one condition to the will. Old Uncle Bruce had a sense of humour and decreed that his nephew should spend at least £100,000 within the first four months, in 'a frivolous manner'.

Bond did not have to think twice about how he might best comply with such an eccentric proviso. Bentley motor cars had always been a passion, and he had sorely resented getting rid of the early models which he had owned, driven and loved. During the last year he had lusted after the brand new Bentley Mulsanne Turbo. When the will was finally through probate, he took himself straight down to Jack Barclay's showrooms in Berkeley Square and ordered the hand-built car – in his old favourite colour, British Racing Green, with a magnolia interior.

One month later, he visited the Rolls-Royce Car Division at Crewe and spent a pleasant day with the Chief Executive. He explained that he wanted no special technology built into the car apart from a small concealed weapon compartment and a long-range telephone which would be provided by the security experts at CCS. The Mulsanne Turbo was delivered in the late spring, and Bond, having put down the full price with the order, was happy to get rid of the remaining £30,000 plus by spending it on friends, mainly female, and himself in a spree of high living such as he had not enjoyed for years.

But 007 was not so easily brought out of the doldrums. He longed for some kind of action – a craving that he tried to curb with too many late nights, the excitement of the gaming tables, and a lukewarm affair with a girl he had known for years; a small romance that sputtered out like a candle flame after a few months. His period of lotus-eating failed miserably to remove the unsettled edgy sense that his life had lost both purpose and direction.

There was one week, in the late spring, when he found some pleasure with the Q Branch Armourer, Major Boothroyd, and his delectable assistant Q'ute, testing a handgun the Service was toying with using on a regular basis. Bond found the ASP 9mm, a combat modification of the 9mm Smith & Wesson, to be one of the most satisfying weapons he had ever used. But then the ASP had been constructed to specifications supplied by the United States Intelligence and Security Services.

In the middle of August, when London was crowded with tourists, and a torpor appeared to hang over the Regent's Park Headquarters, there was a summons from M's secretary, the faithful Miss Moneypenny, and Bond found himself in his chief's office, with Bill Tanner in attendance. It was here, on the ninth floor, overlooking the hot, dusty park, that M surprised Bond by bringing up the matter of the Australian legacy.

Moneypenny was far from her usual, flirtatious self while Bond waited in the outer office. She gave the distinct impression that, whatever the cause of M's summons, the news could not be good. The feeling was heightened once he was allowed into the main office. Bill Tanner was present, and both the Chief-of-Staff and M looked wary, M's eyes not even meeting Bond's and Tanner hardly turning to acknowledge his presence.

'We have a pair of Russian ambulance chasers in town,' M stated baldly and without emphasis once Bond was seated in front of his desk.

'Sir.' There was no other possible response to this opening gambit.

'New boys to us,' M continued. 'No diplomatic cover, French papers, but definitely high quality ambulance chasers.' The Head of Service was talking about Russian operatives whose specific task was to recruit potential informants and double agents.

'You want me to put them on the first aircraft back to Moscow, sir?' Bond's spirits rose a little, for even that simple chore would be better than sitting around the office shuffling papers.

M ignored the offer. Instead he looked at the ceiling. 'Come into money, 007? That's what I hear.'

'A small legacy . . .' Bond found himself almost shocked by M's remark.

M raised his eyebrows quizzically, muttering, 'Small?'

'The ambulance chasers are high-powered professionals.' Bill Tanner spoke from the window. 'They've both had some success in other parts of the world – Washington, for instance – though there's never been hard evidence. Washington and Bonn. These fellows got in very quietly on both occasions, and nobody knew about them until it was too late. They did a lot of damage in Washington. Even more in Bonn.'

'The orders to expel arrived after the birds had flown,' M interjected.

'So, now you know they're here in the UK and you want some solid evidence?' An unpleasant thought had crept into Bond's mind.

Bill Tanner came over, dragging a chair with him so that he could sit close to Bond. 'Fact is, we've got wind at an early stage. We presume they think we don't know about them. Our brothers at Five have been co-operative for once . . .'

'They're here and active then?' Bond tried to remain calm, for it was not like M or Tanner to beat about the bush. 'You want hard evidence?' he asked again.

Tanner took in a deep breath, like a man about to unburden his soul. 'M wants to mount a dangle,' he said quietly.

'Tethered goat. Bait,' M growled.

'Me?' Bond slipped a hand into his breast pocket withdrawing his gunmetal cigarette case.

'By all means,' said M in acknowledgment that Bond might smoke, and he lit one of his H. Simmons specials, bought in bulk from the old shop in the Burlington Arcade where they were still to be had.

'Me?' Bond repeated. 'The tethered goat?'

'Something like that.'

'With respect, sir, that's like talking of a woman being slightly pregnant.' He gave a bleak smile. 'Either I'm to be the bait, or I'm not.'

'Yes.' M cleared his throat, plainly embarrassed by what he was about to suggest. 'Well . . . it really came to us because of your . . . your little windfall.' He stressed the word 'little'.

'I don't see what that's got to do with it . . .'

'Let me put a couple of questions to you.' M fiddled with his pipe. 'How many people know you've, er, come into money?'

'Obviously those with need-to-know in the Service, sir. Apart from that only my solicitor, my late uncle's solicitor and myself . . .'

'Not reported in any newspapers, not bandied about, *not* public knowledge?'

'Certainly not public knowledge, sir.'

M and Tanner exchanged glances. 'You have been living at a somewhat extravagant pace, 007,' said M, scowling.

Bond remained silent, waiting for the news to be laid on him. As he had thought, it was not good.

Tanner took up the conversation. 'You see, James, there's been some talk. Gossip. People notice things and the word around Whitehall is that Commander Bond is living a shade dangerously – gambling, the new Bentley, er . . . ladies, money changing hands . . .'

'So?' Bond was not going to make it any easier for them.

'So, even our gallant allies in Grosvenor Square have been over asking questions – they do, when a senior officer suddenly changes his habits.'

'The Americans think I'm a security risk?' Bond bridled. 'Damned cheek.'

M rapped on the desk. 'Enough of that, 007. They have every right to ask. You *have* been acting the playboy recently, and that kind of thing always makes them suspicious.'

'And if they get touchy, then there's no knowing what thoughts are running through the minds of those watching from Kensington Gardens,' said Tanner with a forced smile.

'Rubbish,' Bond almost spat. 'They know me too well. They'll ferret out the legacy in no time – if they're interested.'

'Oh, they're interested all right,' Tanner continued. 'You haven't noticed anything?'

Bond's brow creased as he shook his head.

'No? Well, why should you? They've been very discreet. Not a twenty-four hour surveillance or anything like that, but our people on the street have reported that you're under observation. Odd days, occasional nights, questions in unlikely places.'

Bond swore silently. He felt foolish. *Even at home, behave as though you're in the field*, they taught. Elementary, and he had not even noticed. 'Where's this leading, then?' he asked, dreading the answer.

'To the dangle.' Tanner gave a half-smile. 'To a small charade, with you as the central character, James.'

Bond nodded. 'Like I said, I'm going to be the bait.'

'It seems resonable enough.' M turned his attention to his pipe. 'The situation is ideal . . .'

This time Bond did explode, voicing his feelings with some force. It was the most stupid ploy he had ever heard of. No recruiting officer from any foreign agency would seriously consider him – and, if any did, their masters would put a blight on it in ten seconds flat. 'You're not really serious about this, are you?' he ended lamely.

'Absolutely, 007. I agree, on the face of it they'll steer clear of you. But we have to look at the facts – they *are* more than interested already . . .'

'Never in a thousand years . . .' Bond started again.

'We've already formulated the plan, 007, and we're proceeding with it. Do I have to remind you that you're under my orders?'

There were no options, and Bond, feeling the whole business was sheer madness, could only sit and listen to the dialogue as M and Tanner outlined the bare bones of the scheme, like a pair of theatrical directors explaining motivation to a rather dull actor.

'At an appropriate moment we haul you in,' said M with a sour smile.

'Enquiry *in camera*,' counterpointed Bill Tanner.

'Making certain the Press are tipped off.'

'Questions in the House.'

'Hints of scandal. Corruption in the Service.'

'And you resign.'

'Giving the impression that, in reality, we've cast you into outer darkness. And if that doesn't lure the ambulance chasers, then there's something else in the wind. Wait and do as I say, 007.'

And so it had happened – though not because of the ambulance chasers, as they had told him. Rumours ran along the corridors of power; there was gossip in the clubs, tattle in the powder rooms of government departments, hints to the Press, hints by the Press, even questions in the House of Commons, and finally the resignation of Commander James Bond.

3

RIOTOUS LIVING

In the month before the Kruxator robbery Bond himself had been following a hedonistic routine. He stayed in bed until noon and ventured forth only in the evenings, to restaurants, clubs and gaming houses, usually with a pretty girl in tow. Since the Paymaster General's lamentable performance in the House, attempting to make light of certain scandals associated with one of the Foreign Office's field operators and to dismiss Opposition charges of a security cover-up, the Press had, perhaps surprisingly, hardly approached Bond again. He had no contact at all with his former employers. In fact, they went out of their way to avoid him. One evening he found himself at the Inn on the Park seated only two tables from Anne Reilly, the attractive and talented assistant to the Armourer in Q Branch. Bond caught her eye and smiled but she merely looked through him as though he did not exist.

Then, towards the end of April, around noon one mild, bright Thursday, the telephone rang in Bond's flat. Bond, who had been shaving, grabbed at the handset, as though he would have liked to strangle the trilling.

'Yes?' he growled.

'Oh!' The voice was female, and surprised. 'Is that 59 Dean Street? The Record Shop?'

'It's not 59 anything.' Bond did not even smile.

'But I'm sure I dialled 734 8777 . . .'

'Well, you didn't get it.' He slammed the receiver back, irritated by what appeared to be a misrouted call.

Later in the afternoon, he telephoned his date, a favourite blonde stewardess with British Airways, to cancel their evening out. Instead of dinner for two at the Connaught, Bond went alone to Veeraswamy's, that most excellent Indian restaurant in Swallow Street, where he ate a chicken vindaloo with all the trimmings, lingered over his coffee, then paid the bill and left on the dot of nine-fifteen. The magnificent uniformed and bearded doorman gave him a quivering salute, then loudly hailed a cab. Bond tipped the doorman and gave the driver his home address, but at the top of St James's he paid off the taxi and set out on foot, to follow an apparently aimless route, turning into side streets, crossing roads suddenly, doubling back on himself a number of times, loitering at corners, making certain he was not being followed.

Eventually, clinging to this devious routine, he ended up in a doorway near St Martin's Lane. For two minutes Bond stood looking up at a lighted window across the road. At precisely ten o'clock the oblong of light turned black, then lit again, went black, lit and stayed on.

Quickly Bond crossed the road. He disappeared through another doorway, took a narrow flight of stairs, went across a landing and up four more steps to a door labelled *Rich Photography Ltd. Models available.* When he pressed the small button to the right of the lintel the chimes associated with a well-known brand of cosmetics ding-donged from far away inside. There were faint footsteps and the click of bolts being drawn.

The door opened to reveal Bill Tanner who nodded, indicating that Bond should enter. He followed Tanner along a small passage, its paintwork peeling and with a cloying smell of cheap scent hanging in the air, and through the door at the far end. The room was very small and cluttered. A bed partially masked by a hideously patterned coverlet stood in one corner, and a mangy teddy bear lounged on a bright orange, heart-shaped imitation silk nightdress case. A small wardrobe faced the bed, its door half open, displaying a pathetic row of women's clothes. The tiny dressing table was crammed with bottles and jars of cosmetics. Above a popping gas fire, a print of *The Green Lady* looked down from a plastic frame upon a pair of easy chairs which would not have been out of place in a child's Wendy house.

'Come in, 007. Glad to see you can do simple mathematics.' The figure in one of the chairs turned, and Bond found himself looking into the familiar cold grey eyes of his Head of Service.

Tanner closed the door and crossed to a table on which were set several bottles and glasses.

'Good to see you, sir,' Bond said with a smile, holding out a hand. 'Seven and three equals ten. Even I can manage that.'

'Nobody in tow?' the Chief-of-Staff asked anxiously, sidling towards the window which Bond had viewed from the far side of the street.

'Not unless they've got a team of a hundred or so footpads and about twenty cars on me. The traffic's as thick as treacle tonight. Always bad on Thursdays – late night shopping, and the commuters staying up to meet their wives and girlfriends.'

The telephone gave a good old-fashioned ring and Tanner got to it in two strides.

'Yes,' he said, then, again, 'Yes . . . Good . . . Right.' Replacing the receiver, he looked up with a smile. 'He's clear, sir. All the way.'

'I told you . . .' Bond began, but Tanner cut him short with an invitation to take a gin and tonic with them. Bond scowled, shaking his head. 'I've had enough alcohol to float several small ships in the past few weeks . . .'

'So we all noticed,' M grunted.

'Your instructions, sir. I could remind you that I said at the outset nothing would come of it. Nobody in our business would even begin to believe I'd left the Service, just like that. The silence has been deafening.'

M grunted again. 'Sit down, 007. Sit down and listen. The silence has not been so deafening. On the contrary, the isle is full of noises, only you have been on a different frequency. I'm afraid we've kept you in the dark, but it was necessary – that is, until we had established to the various intelligence communities that you were *persona non grata* as far as we're concerned. Forget what we told you during our last meeting. Now we have the real target. Look at this picture – and at this, and this.'

Like an experienced poker player, M laid out three photographs, of one man and two women.

'The man,' he said at last, 'is presumed dead. His name was Dr Jay Autem Holy.' M's finger touched one photograph, then moved on to the next. 'This lady is his widow, and this' – the finger prodded towards the third photograph – 'this is the same lady. Looks so different that should her husband come back from the dead, which is on the cards, he would never recognise her.' M picked up the final photograph. 'She will give you the details. In fact, she'll give you a little training as well. She answers to the name of Proud. Persephone Proud. Ms.'

Proud was plump, with mousy brown hair, thick-lensed spectacles, thin lips and a sharp nose too big for her rather chubby face. At least that was how she looked in the photograph taken some years ago when she was married to Jay Autem Holy. M maintained that Bond would not recognise her now either. That did not surprise him when he studied the third photograph.

'You're sending me on another course?' Bond mused rather absently without looking up.

'Something like that. She's waiting for you now.'

'Yes?'

'In Monaco. Monte Carlo. Hotel de Paris. Now listen carefully, 007. There's a good deal for you to absorb, and I want you on the road early next week. You must, naturally, still consider yourself as one cast into outer darkness. But this is what we, together with our American cousins, planned from the start.'

M talked earnestly for about fifteen minutes, allowing no

interruptions, before Bond was escorted through another elaborate security routine to get him safely clear of the building and on his way home in a taxi without being followed. Not for the first time, Bond had been given another life, a double identity. But of the many dubious parts he had played for his country, this was to appear more than any as a role of dishonour.

4

PROUD PERCY

Bond particularly enjoyed the drive through France, down to the South, for it was the first time he had been able to let the huge Mulsanne Turbo off the leash. The car seemed to revel in the business of doing its job with perfection. Bentley had certainly produced another true thoroughbred from their stable. The Mulsanne pushed its long, elegant snout forward, and then, like some runner in peak condition, gathered itself together, effortlessly reaching well in excess of the 100 miles per hour mark and eating up road without fuss or noise, as if it were floating over the tarmac on a silent cushion of air.

Bond had left London early on the Monday morning, and he had been told Ms Proud would be in the Casino each evening, from the Tuesday, between ten and eleven.

At a little after six on Tuesday the Mulsanne slid into Monaco's Place Casino, and up to the entrance of the Hotel de Paris. It was a splendid, clear spring evening, with hardly a breath of wind to stir the palm trees in the gardens which front the Grand Casino. As he switched off the ignition, Bond checked that the small hidden weapon compartment below the polished wooden dashboard to the right of the wheel, was locked and that the safety key was turned on the powerful Super 1000 telephone housed between the front seats. Stepping out, he glanced around the Place, nostrils filling with a mixture of mimosa, heavy French tobacco and the soft sea air.

Monte Carlo, like the neighbouring cities and towns along the

Côte d'Azur, had a smell that was all its own. Bond reckoned a fortune could be made if someone could only bottle it, to provide nostalgic memories for those who had known the principality in its heyday. For the one-time gambling legend of Europe was no longer the great romantic fairytale place remembered by those who had won, and lost, fortunes and hearts there. The package holiday, the weekend break and the charter flight had put an end to that. Monaco managed to keep up its veneer of sophistication only through the presence of its royal family and the high prices speculators, hoteliers, restaurateurs and shopkeepers charged. Even those had not created a safe buffer against some of the more garish encroachments of the 1980s. On his last visit, Bond had been horrified to find one-armed bandits installed in the exclusive Salles Privées of the Casino. Now he would not be surprised if there were space invader games there as well.

His room faced the sea and, before taking a shower and preparing for the evening, he stood on the balcony, looking out at the twinkling lights and sipping a martini. For a moment he wondered if it were possible to recapture the sounds and laughter of former, brighter days.

After a modest dinner – chilled consommé, grilled sole, and a *mousse au chocolat* – he went down to check the car, then walked over to the Casino, paid the entrance fee to admit him to the fabled Salles Privées and bought 50,000 francs' worth of chips – around £4,000 sterling.

There was play at only one of the tables. As Bond crossed the floor, he saw Persephone Proud for the first time. M had understated the case when he said even her husband would not recognise her. Bond, who had hardly credited the 'after' photograph, as M had called it, found it difficult to believe that this woman, undeniably the one from that photograph, could ever have been either plump or mousy.

She stood, bare-shouldered, her back against the bar, a tall, almost willowy figure, head tilted, small breasts thrusting into relief against the flimsy material of her blue dress. Long ash-blonde hair just touched the tanned skin at the nape of her neck, and her light blue-grey eyes, twinkling with amusement, were intent on the play at the table. A half-smile hovered around her mouth, full lips having replaced the original, while the angular nose was now almost a snub.

Fascinating, Bond thought. Fascinating to see what strict diet, a nose job, contact lenses and a dedicated course of beauty treatment could accomplish.

He did not pause on his way to the table, where he took a seat, acknowledging the croupier, and studying the game for three turns before dropping 25,000 francs on *Impair*.

The croupier called an almost ritual *'Faites vos jeux'*. All eyes watched, as the little ball bounced into the spinning wheel.

'Rien ne va plus.' Bond glanced at the three other players – a smooth, American-looking man, late forties, blue-jowled and with the steely look of a professional gambler; a woman in her early seventies, he judged, dressed in last season's fashions; and a heavy-set Chinese whose face would never give away his age. Everyone followed the wheel now as the ball bounced twice and settled into a slot. *'Dix-sept, rouge, impair et manque,'* the croupier intoned in that particular plainchant of the tables. Seventeen, red, odd and low.

The rake swung efficiently over the green baize, taking in the house winnings, and pushing out plaques to the winners, including Bond, whose *Impair* bet had netted him even money. At the call, he again placed 25,000 on *Impair*. Once more he won, eleven coming up. *Impair* for a third time, and the ball rolled into fifteen. In three turns of the wheel, Bond had made 75,000 francs. He was playing the easy way, high stakes for even returns. The other players were betting complex patterns – *A Cheval, Carré*, and *Colonne* – which made for higher odds. Bond pushed the whole of his 75,000 francs on to *Pair* and fourteen – red came up. Stake plus 75,000 francs. Time to call it a night. He flipped a 5,000 franc chip across the table, muttering *'Pour les employés,'* and pushed back the chair. There was a little squeal as it touched the girl's legs, and Bond felt liquid run down his left cheek where her drink spilled. It was a natural enough incident, for the Englishman had not sensed her standing behind him. The move had been carefully pre-arranged far away in London, in the safe flat near St Martin's Lane.

'I'm terribly sorry . . . *Pardon, madame, je . . .*'

'It's okay, I speak English.' The voice was pitched low, the accent clear and without nasality. 'It was my fault, I shouldn't have been standing so close. The game was very . . .'

'Well, at least let me get you a fresh drink.'

Bond finished drying his face and took her elbow, steering her towards the small bar. One of the dinner-jacketed security men smiled as he watched them go. Hadn't he seen women pick up men like this many times? No harm in it, as long as the women were straight, and this one was an American visitor. Silently he wished them luck.

'Mr . . . ?' She raised her champagne cocktail to his.

'James Bond. My friends call me James.'

'And mine call me Percy. Persephone Proud's too much of a mouthful.'

Bond's eyes smiled over the rim of the glass. 'Percy Proud,' he said, an eyebrow cocked, 'I'll drink to that.'

Percy was a relaxed young woman, an easy communicator blessed with a sense of humour, and of the ridiculous.

'Okay, James . . .' they were at last seated in her room at the Hotel de Paris, armed with champagne cocktails '. . . down to details. How much *have* you been told?'

'Very little.' *She'll give you the fine print*, M had said. *Play up to her; trust her; let her teach you. She knows more about all this than anyone.*

'You've seen this picture?' She extracted a small photograph from her handbag. 'I just have to show it to you and then destroy it. I don't want to be caught with it on me.'

The photograph was a smaller print of the one they had shown Bond in the St Martin's Lane flat.

'Jay Autem Holy,' Bond said. The man looked very tall, his thinning hair failing to disguise a domed head, and he had a large, beaky nose.

'*Doctor* Jay Autem Holy,' she corrected.

'Deceased. And you are the widow – though I wouldn't have recognised you after some of the photos I've seen.'

She gave a quick, infectious giggle. 'There have been some changes made.'

'I'll say. The other identity would not have been attractive in black . . . You'd look good in anything.'

'Flattery could get you everywhere, James Bond. But I don't really think Mrs Jay Autem Holy ever needed widow's weeds. You see, he never died.'

'Tell me.'

She began with the story already told by M. Over a decade before, while Dr Jay Autem Holy had been working solely for the Pentagon, a US Marine Corps Grumman Mohawk aircraft had crashed into the Grand Canyon. Dr Holy and a General Joseph ('Rolling Joe') Zwingli were the only passengers.

'You already know that Jay Autem was way ahead of his time,' she said. 'A computer whizz-kid long before most people had heard of computers. He worked on very advanced programming for the Pentagon. The airplane went down in a most inaccessible place – wreckage dumped deep into a gully. No bodies were ever recovered, and Jay Autem had a nice bundle of significant computer tapes with him when he went. Naturally they were not recovered either. He was working on a portable battle-training program for senior officers, and had almost perfected a computerised system for anticipating enemy movements in the field. His work was literally invaluable.'

'And the General?'

'Rolling Joe? A nut. A much-decorated and brave nut. Believed the United States had gone to the dogs – the commie dogs. Said openly there should be a change in the political system, that the army should take control. He figured politicians had sold out, morals had gone to pieces, people had to be *made* to care.'

Bond nodded. 'And I gather Dr Holy had a nickname – like Rolling Joe was Zwingli's nickname.'

She laughed again. 'They called Zwingli "Rolling Joe" because in World War Two he had this habit of air-testing his B17 Flying Fortress by rolling it at a thousand feet.'

'And Dr Holy?' he prompted.

'His colleagues, and some of his friends, called him "The Holy Terror". He could be a tough boss.' Percy paused, before adding, 'And a tough husband.'

'Late husband.' Bond gave her a close, unblinking look and watched her drain the last of her champagne cocktail and place the glass carefully on a side table as she slowly shook her head.

'Oh no,' she said softly. 'Jay Autem Holy did not die in that airplane wreck. A few people have known that for some years. Now there's proof.'

'Proof? Where?' He led her towards the moment for which M had prepared him.

'Right on your own doorstep, James. Deep in the heart of rural England. Oxfordshire. And there's more to it than that. You remember the Kruxator robbery in London? And the £20 million gold bullion job?'

Bond nodded.

'Also the £2 billion hijack? The British Airways 747 taking foreign currencies from the official printers in England to their respective countries?'

'Of course.'

'You remember what those crimes had in common, James?'

He waved his gunmetal cigarette case at Percy, who declined with an almost imperceptible gesture of the hand. Bond was surprised to find the case being returned to his pocket unopened. His forehead creased.

'All large sums,' he said. 'Well-planned . . . Wait a minute, didn't Scotland Yard say they could almost be computerised crimes?'

'That's it. You have the answer.'

'Percy – ' there was an edge of puzzlement in Bond's voice – 'what are you suggesting?'

'That Dr Jay Autem Holy is alive and well, and living in a small village called Nun's Cross, just north of Banbury in your lovely Oxfordshire. Remember Banbury, James? The place where you can ride a cock-horse to?' Her lips tightened a little. 'Well, that's where he is. Planning criminal operations, and probably terrorist ones as well, by computer simulations.'

'Evidence?'

'Well . . .' Again a pause. 'To say that no bodies were recovered in the airplane is not quite true. They got out the pilot's remains. There were no other bodies. Intelligence, security and police agencies have been searching for Jay Autem Holy ever since.'

'And suddenly they found him in Oxfordshire?'

'Almost by chance, yes. One of your Special Branch men was in that area on a completely different case. He was on to a pair of well-known London crooks.'

'And they led him to . . . ?'

Percy got up and slowly began to pace the room.

'They led him to a small computer simulations company called Gunfire Simulations, in the village of Nun's Cross, and there he sees a face from the files. So he goes back and checks. The face is Dr Jay Autem Holy's. Only now he calls himself Professor Jason St John-Finnes – pronounced Sinjon-Finesse: finesse, as in the game of bridge. The name of the house is Endor.'

'As in Witch of?'

'Right.'

Percy paused in her pacing and leaned on the back of Bond's armchair, her arm brushing his ear. He could not at that moment bring himself to turn his head and look up into the face above his shoulder.

'They even have chummy little weekend war games parties there and a lot of strange people turn up,' Percy continued. She moved away and dropped on to a couch, drawing her long slender legs up under her.

'Trouble was, none of this happened to be news to the American Service. You see, they've been keeping an eye on that situation for some time. Even infiltrated it, without telling anyone.'

Bond smiled. 'That would please my people no end. There are rules about operating on other countries' soil and . . .'

'As I understand it,' Percy interrupted in a husky, drawling voice, 'there were what is known as frank and open discussions.'

'I'll bet!' Bond thought for a moment. 'Are you telling me that Jay Autem Holy – strongly prized by the Pentagon and missing, believed dead – just managed to settle in this village, Nun's Cross, without benefit of disguise or cover, except for some new identity papers?'

Percy stretched out her legs and laid back almost full length on the couch, brushing the floor languidly with her hand.

'Not an easy man to disguise,' she said. 'But yes, that's exactly what he's done. Mind you he rarely goes out, he's hardly ever seen in the village. His so-called wife deals personally with business, and those he genuinely employs just think he's eccentric – which he is. A great deal of ingenuity and a lot of money went into fixing up Jay Autem's hideaway.'

Slowly, many of the things M had said back in London started to make sense. As though dawn had suddenly broken, Bond said, 'And I'm the one who's supposed to join that happy band of brothers?'

'You've got it in one.'

'And just how am I supposed to do that? Walk in and say, Hi there, my name's James Bond, the famous renegade intelligence officer: I'm looking for a job?'

It was Bond's turn to get up and pace the room.

'Something like that,' Percy drawled softly.

'Good God!' Bond's face tightened in anger. 'Of all the hare-brained . . . Why would he want to employ me, anyway?'

'He wouldn't.' She gave a flicker of a smile and sat up, suddenly very alert and earnest. 'He's got enough staff to run the Gunfire Simulations business all legal and above board. And *are* they screened! It makes the British positive vetting look like a kid's crossword puzzle. Believe me, I know. He has to be certain, because that side of things is absolutely straight.' She took a little breath, turning her head slightly, like a singer swinging away from the microphone. 'No, James, he wouldn't think of employing you but there are people he works with who just might find you a great temptation. That's what your people are banking on.'

'Mad. Absolute madness! How?' Bond was really angry again.

'James,' she said soothingly, standing up and taking both his hands in hers. 'You have friends at the court of King St John-Finnes – well, an acquaintance anyhow. Freddie Fortune. The naughty Lady Freddie.'

'Oh Lord!' Bond dropped Percy's hands and swung aside. Once, some years ago, Bond had made the error of cultivating the young woman Percy had just mentioned. In a way he had even courted her, until he discovered that Lady Freddie Fortune, darling of the gossip columnists, suffered from a somewhat slapdash political education, which had placed her slightly to the left of Fidel Castro.

'You too will have to study, James. That's why you're going to be here, with me. To get an entrée into Endor you must know something about the job they do at Gunfire Simulations. How much do you really know about computers?'

Bond gave a sheepish smile. 'If you put it like that, the technicalities only.'

Had he been asked, computers were the last thing he wanted to discuss just then with the strangely alluring and unsettling Persephone Proud.

5

WAR GAME

With a lucidity born of his years in the Service, Bond outlined to Percy the way a microcomputer works, as they both sauntered about the room in almost a ritual dance, carefully avoiding one another. A complex electronic tool designed to perform particular tasks when a series of commands are read into its two memories, he recited tonelessly, like a schoolboy reeling off Latin declensions to an indulgent master. A machine which could keep records and work out financial problems one minute, process data the next, receive and transmit information over thousands of miles in a matter of seconds; which would design your new house, or allow you to play complicated games, make music, or display moving graphics. A miracle with an ever-growing memory, but only as good as the program it is given.

'I know the theory – just,' Bond said with a smile, 'but I haven't a clue how it's all done by the programmer.'

'That, as I understand it from your wonderful old boss, is the main reason we're here,' Percy retorted. Bond was mildly surprised to hear M spoken of as his wonderful old boss. 'My job is to teach you programming language, with special reference to the kind of thing my dark angel of an ex-husband used to do, and probably is doing right now. Oh, yes, he is an ex. Dead, missing, whatever, I made sure it was legal.'

'Would that be difficult?' Bond asked with a show of feigned innocence. 'Learning to program, I mean.'

'Depends on aptitude. It's like swimming or riding a bicycle.

Once you've got the knack it becomes second nature. Mind you, we're up against a particular kind of genius when it comes to Jay Autem Holy. I'm going to have to tell you a lot about *him*. Seriously, though, it's simply like learning a new language, or how to read music.'

Percy walked over to the closet and hauled out a pair of large customised cases heavily embellished with coded security locks. Between them they contained a large, sophisticated micro-computer, several types of disk drive, and three metal boxes which, when opened, revealed disks of differing sizes and quality. She asked Bond to move the television set so that she could plug in the micro. The keyboard was twice the size of that on an electronic typewriter. Percy talked as she set up the equipment. This was the same micro, she said, as she guessed Jay Autem would be using now. Bond had already noticed that she referred to Dr Holy simply as Jay Autem or the Holy Terror.

'When he went missing his own micro disappeared with him – or, should I say, at the same time. I guess he had it stashed away somewhere safe. In those days we were just beginning to see the full development of the microcompressor – you know, the chip that put a whole roomful of computer circuits on to a 5mm-square piece of silicon. When he built his own machine we were still mainly using tapes. Since then there've been so many de-velopments, and things have become much smaller, but I've tried to keep pace with the technology. I rebuilt his Terror Six – that's what he called his machine – changing his original design, doing my best to keep one jump ahead, as he would have done.'

Bond stood peering over her shoulder as she made final adjust-ments.

'This,' she waved a hand at the keyboard, 'is my equivalent of what would now be the Terror Twelve. Since Jay Autem went, the chips have gotten smaller, but the big leap forward has been the incredible advance in the amount of memory a little thing like this can contain. That, and the way more realistic pictures –

real video – can be used in the kind of programs he's interested in.'

'And what kind of programs are those, Percy?'

'Well – ' she selected a disk from one of the boxes, switched on a drive, inserted the disk and powered up the machine – 'I can show you the kind of thing which used to fascinate him when he was doing work for the Pentagon. Then we can take it a stage further.'

The television screen had come alive, the disk drive whirred and rasped, and a series of rapid beeps emanated from the speaker. The drive continued to sound after the staccato beeps finally stopped and the screen cleared, showing a detailed map of the border between East and West Germany – the district around Kassel: NATO country.

Unaccountably Bond suddenly felt hot and flushed. He started to reach a hand out to Percy's shoulder, but changed to loosen his tie as she drew a heavy black joystick from one of her cases and plugged it into the keyboard, pressing the S key. Immediately a bright rectangle appeared on the map, which Bond saw was as clear as a piece of printed cartography.

'Okay, this may look like some weird game to you, but I promise you, it's a very advanced training aid.'

Percy operated the joystick and the rectangle slid across the screen, moving the map as it reached the outer perimeter, so that it scrolled up and down. The entire area covered was about eighty square miles of border and below it on the screen was a blank oblong blue space.

'I type in co-ordinates and we go immediately to that section on the map.' Percy suited action to word, and the map jumped on the screen, the rectangle staying in place. 'Now we can look at what's going on in a smaller area.' She positioned the rectangle over a village about a mile from the border and pressed the trigger on the joystick. Bond had suddenly become aware of the perfume Percy was wearing but couldn't decide what it was. He jerked his mind back to the matter in hand.

It was as if a zoom lens had been applied to the screen, for now he could see detail – roads, trees, houses, rocks and fields. Among this detail Bond could pick out at least six tanks and four troop carriers, while a pair of helicopters sat hidden behind buildings, and three Harrier aircraft could be defined on pads shielded by trees.

'We have to assume that some form of non-nuclear hostility exists.'

Percy was typing commands into the micro, asking for information, first on NATO forces. The tanks, troop carriers, helicopters and Harriers blinked in turn, as their designated call-signs and strength ribboned out on the lower part of the screen. Percy noted the call-signs on a pad at her elbow and then typed a command for information about Warsaw Pact forces in this tiny area. They appeared to be facing at least two companies of infantry, with armoured support.

'It'll only give you available information, the kind of thing intelligence and reconnaissance would actually have.' Percy watched as the screen flashed up known positions, with data concerning the enemy running out on the blue space below.

Bond could not take his eyes from the soft curl of her hair on an almost exposed shoulder as she began to input orders. Two of the Harriers moved off, as though flying in to attack the enemy armour. At the same time, she activated the NATO tanks and troop carriers.

Individual responses from the tank and infantry commanders came up on the screen, while the tiny vehicles moved to her bidding, the tanks suddenly coming under attack, indicated by shell bursts on the screen and audible crumps and whines. Bond stooped slightly for a closer look, and found himself glancing sideways at Percy's face, profiled and absorbed alongside his. He looked quickly back at the screen.

The action, controlled throughout by Percy, lasted for almost twenty minutes, during which time she was able to gain a small superiority over the enemy forces with the loss of three tanks, one helicopter, a Harrier and just under one hundred men.

Bond stood back a pace behind Percy. He had found the whole operation fascinating. He asked if this kind of thing were used by the military.

'This is only a simple computer TEWT.' Percy was talking about a Tactical Exercise Without Troops, a technique used in training officers and NCOs. 'In the old days, as you know, they did TEWTs with boards, tables, sand trays and models. Now all you need is a micro. This is very simple, but you should see the advanced games they use at staff colleges.'

'And Dr Holy was programming this kind of thing for the Pentagon?' For the first time Bond noticed a little mole on Percy's neck.

'This, and more. When he disappeared, Jay Autem was into some exceptionally advanced stuff. Not only training but specialist programs, where the computer is given all the possible options and works out the one most likely to be taken by an opposing power under a particular set of circumstances.'

'And now? Given that he really is still alive . . .'

'Oh, he's alive, James.' She flushed suddenly. 'I've seen him. Don't doubt it. He's the one I've already told you about – Jason St John-Finnes, of Nun's Cross, Oxfordshire. I should know. After all, I was his watchdog for three and a half lousy years . . .'

'Watchdog?' Her eyes really were the most incredible colour, a subtle shade of grey-blue that changed according to the light.

Percy looked away, biting her lip in mock shame. 'Oh, didn't they tell you? I married the bastard under orders. I'm a Company lady – from Langley. Marriage to Dr Holy was an assignment. How else would I know the inside of this op?'

'He wasn't trusted then?' Bond tried not to show surprise, even though the idea of a CIA employee being instructed to marry in order to keep surveillance on her husband appalled him.

'At that time, with his contacts – he had many friends among the scientific community in Russia and the Eastern Bloc – they couldn't afford to trust him. And they were right.'

'You think he's working for the KGB now?'

'No.' She went to the small chiller to get another bottle of champagne. 'No, Jay Autem worked for Jay Autem and nobody else. At least I discovered that about him.' Passing another glass to Bond, she added, 'There are almost certainly Soviet connections in what he's doing now, but it'll be on a freelance basis. Jay Autem knows his business, but he's really dedicated only to money. Politics is another matter.'

'So what sort of thing do you reckon he's doing?' Bond caught another strong whiff of that strange perfume which he would always now associate with Percy.

'As they say, James, that's for him to know and you to find out. And it's my job to teach you how. Tomorrow morning we start in earnest. Eight-thirty suit you?'

'Hardly worth my going back to my own room.' He glanced casually at his watch.

'I know, but you're going all the same. I'm to teach you all I can about how to prepare the kind of programs Jay Autem writes, *and* give you a course on how to break into his programs, should you be lucky enough to get your hands on one.'

Percy took hold of his wrist and reached up to kiss him gently on the cheek. Bond moved closer, but Percy stepped away, wagging a finger.

'That's a no-no, James. But I'm a good teacher, and if you prove to be a diligent pupil, I have ways of rewarding you that you never dreamed of when you were at school. Eight-thirty sharp. Okay?'

'You guarantee results, Proud Percy?'

'I guarantee to teach you, Bond James,' she said with a wicked grin, 'and about computer programming as well.'

Promptly at eight-thirty the next morning, Bond knocked on her door, one arm hidden behind his back. When she opened up, he thrust out his hand to give her a large rosy apple.

'For the teacher,' he said with a broad smile.

It was the only joke of the day, for Percy Proud proved to be a hard and dedicated taskmaster.

6

HOLY CODE

The training took a little less than a month and was a tribute to Persephone Proud's teaching skill. Her pupil's capabilities were taxed to the limit. The task had been equivalent to learning a new language and several complicated dialects as well. Indeed, Bond could not remember a time when he had been forced to call so heavily on his mental reserves, to focus his mind, like a burning glass, on the subject at hand.

They quickly established a routine, which seldom varied. For the first few days they started at eight-thirty each morning, but, as the late nights began to take their toll, this was modified to ten o'clock. They would work until one o'clock, take lunch in a nearby bar, walking there and back, then work again until five.

Each evening at seven they would go down to Le Bar, the Hotel de Paris's famous meeting place, where, it is said, the wrists and necks of the ladies put the Carrier showcases to shame.

If they intended to stay in Monaco for the evening they would dine at the hotel, but they could be seen at L'Oasis in La Napoule when the Cannes Casino took their fancy, sampling the latest tempting dish invented by the master chef, Louis Outhier. Sometimes they would eat a more austere meal at the Negresco in Nice, or even in La Réserve at Beaulieu, or – on occasion – at the modest Le Galion in the Menton port of Garavan. The meal was always a prelude to a night at the tables. *Don't go invisible,*

M had instructed. *You are bait, and it would be a mistake to forget it. If they are trawling there, let them catch you.*

So the Bentley Mulsanne Turbo slid its silent way along the coast roads each evening, and the tanned, assured Englishman with his willowy elegant American companion, became familiar figures in the gambling landscape of the Côte d'Azur.

Bond played only the wheel, and then conservatively – though he tended to double up on bets, plunging heavily on some evenings, coming away thousands to the good on others. Mainly he worked to a system, using big money on the *Pair, Impair, Manque* and *Passe* which paid evens, only occasionally changing to a *Carré* – covering four numbers at odds of just over eight to one. Within the first week, he was the equivalent of a few thousand pounds sterling to the good and knew the various casinos were watching with interest. No casino, even with the reputation of those along that once glittering coast, is happy about a regular who plays systematically and wins.

Most nights, Percy and Bond were back at the hotel between three and three-thirty in the morning. Sometimes it was earlier – even one o'clock – giving them a chance to do another hour's work before getting a good sleep before starting all over again.

From time to time, during those weeks, they would not return until dawn. Driving the coast roads with the windows open to breathe the morning air, they feasted their eyes on the greenery of palm and plane trees, the cacti and climbing flowers around the summer homes of the wealthy, their swimming pools fed by spouting marble dolphins. On those occasions they would get back to the hotel in time to smell the first coffee of the day – one of the most satisfying aromas in the world, Bond thought.

The hotel staff considered it all very romantic, the attractive American lady and the wealthy Englishman, so lucky at the tables, and in love. Nobody would have dreamed of disturbing the love-birds.

The truth concerning their enclosed life in Percy's room was far removed from the fantasies of chambermaids and porters, at least for the first couple of weeks.

Percy began by teaching Bond how to flowchart a program – to draw out, in a kind of graph, exactly what he wanted the program to do. This he mastered in a matter of forty-eight hours, after which the serious business of learning the computer language, Basic, began. There were extra lessons on the use of graphics and sound. Towards the end of the second week, Bond started to learn various dialects of Basic, gradually grasping the essentials of further, more complex languages like Machine Code, the high-level Pascal, and Forth.

Even in their spare time, they spoke of little else but the job in hand, though usually with special reference to Jay Autem Holy, and it did not take long for Bond to glean that Holy used his own hybrid program language, which Percy referred to as Holy Code.

'It's one of Jay Autem's main strengths as far as protecting his programs is concerned,' Percy told him over dinner. 'He's still using the same system, and the games being produced by Gunfire Simulations are quite inaccessible to other programmers. He always said that if security were necessary – and by God he believed in it – the simplest protection is the best. He has an almost perfect little routine at the start of all his games programs that's quite unreadable by anyone who wants to copy or get into the disk. It's exactly the same code he used to put on to his Pentagon work. Anyone trying to copy or list turns the disk into rubbish.'

Bond insisted on talking about Dr Holy whenever he was given the opportunity, to seek out as much as he could about the man's strengths and weaknesses before meeting him. There could certainly be no better instructor than Percy in this area.

'He looks like a great angry hawk. Well, you've seen the photographs.' They were dining in the hotel. 'Outward appearances are not to be trusted, though. If I hadn't been on a specific job, I could so easily have fallen for him. In fact, in some ways I did. There were often times when I hoped he'd prove to be straight.'

She looked pensive, and for a moment it was as though she did not see Bond, or the magnificent dining hall dating back to the Third Empire and undoubtedly the best restaurant in the principality.

'He has amazing powers of concentration. That knack of being able to close off the rest of the world and allow his own work to become the only reality. You know how dangerous that can be.'

Bond reflected on his own past encounters with the kind of madness that turned men into devils.

It was after this particular dinner, towards the end of the second week, that something happened to change the even tenor of Bond's emotions for some time to come.

'So, are we playing the Salles Privées tonight, or shall we jaunt?' Percy asked.

Bond decided on a trip along the coast to the small casino in Menton, and they left soon afterwards.

The gaming itself did not make it a night to remember, though Bond left with a few thousand francs bulging in his wallet. As they pulled away from the casino to take the road through Roquebrune-Cap-Martin and so back to Monaco, he caught the lights of a car drawing away directly behind him. He knew there had been a car there, but he had seen nobody getting into it. Immediately he told Percy to tighten her seatbelt.

'Trouble?' she asked, but betrayed no sign of nervousness.

'I'm going to find out,' he said as he accelerated, letting the big car glide steadily into the nineties, holding well into the side of the narrow road, praying the police were not around, then thinking perhaps it would be better if they were.

The lights of the car behind remained visible in the driving mirror. When Bond was forced to slow – for that road twists and turns before reaching the long stretch of two-lane highway – it came even closer. It was hard to tell if anything was wrong.

Plenty of traffic used this route, though it was late and the season had yet to get under way.

The car tailing them was a white Citroën, its distinctive rounded bonnet clearly visible behind the lowered headlights. It stuck like a limpet, a discreet distance behind. Bond wondered whether it was just some young Frenchman or Italian wanting to race or show off to a girlfriend. Yet the prickling sensation around the back of his neck told him this was a more sinister challenge.

They came off the two-lane stretch like a rocket, with Bond stabbing at the big footbrake in order to drop speed quickly. From there the road into Monaco was not only narrow but closed in on both sides by rockface or houses, leaving little room for manoeuvre. He took the next bend at about sixty miles per hour. Percy made a little audible intake of breath. As he heard her, Bond saw the obstruction. Another car pulled over to the right, but was still in the Bentley's road space, its hazard lights winking like a dragon's eyes. To the left and hardly moving, blocking most of the remaining space, was an old and decrepit lorry, wheezing as though about to suffer a complete collapse. Bond yelled for Percy to hang on, jabbed hard at the brake, and slewed the Bentley first left, then right, in an attempt to slalom his way between the vehicles. Halfway through the right-hand skid, it was plain they would not make it. The Bentley's engine howled as he pushed the lever from automatic drive to low-range, taking the engine down to first.

They were both pressed hard against the restraining straps of their seatbelts as the heavy car came to a halt, the speed dropping from fifty-five almost to zero in the blink of an eye. They were angled across the road, with the oncoming car jamming their right side and the elderly lorry backing slightly on the left. Two men jumped down from the lorry, and another pair materialised from the shadows surrounding the parked car as the white Citroën boxed them in neatly from behind.

'Doors!' Bond shouted, slamming his hand against his door

lock control, knowing his warning was more of a precaution than anything else, for the central locking system should be in operation. At least three of the men now approaching the Bentley appeared to be armed with axes.

Bond realised as he reached for the hidden pistol compartment catch that his action was only a reflex. If he operated the electric window to use the weapon, they would have a route in. In fact, they could get in anyway, for even a car built like his would eventually collapse under efficiently wielded axes.

The Bentley Mulsanne Turbo is a little over six and a half feet wide. Bond's was not quite at right angles across the road. The Citroën behind, he judged, was within a foot of his rear bumper, but the Bentley's weight would compensate for that. Ahead, the car with its hazard lights blinking was a couple of inches from his door, the lorry some three inches from the bonnet. Directly in front, eight feet or so away, the roadside reached up a sloping rock face. The Bentley's engine had not stalled and still gave out its low grumble.

Holding his foot hard on the brake pedal, Bond adjusted the wheel and, as one of the assailants came abreast of his window, placing himself between the Mulsanne and the parked car, raising both hands to bring down the axe, Bond slid the gear lever into reverse, and lifted his foot smartly off the brake.

The Bentley slid backwards, fast. There was a judder as they hit the Citroën, and a yelp of pain from the man about to try and force entry with his axe. Thrown to one side, he had been crushed between the Bentley and the parked car.

With a quick movement of his right hand, Bond now slid the automatic gear into drive. He had, maybe, an extra six inches to play with. His foot bore gently down on the accelerator. The car eased forward. The screaming attacker on their right was once again crushed as the Bentley straightened up, then gathered speed and headed for the small gap.

The steering on the Mulsanne Turbo is so light and accurate that Bond did not have to wrench at the wheel. Using a very

light touch of his fingers, he eased the Bentley into the narrow
gap between lorry and car. More control to the left. Straight.
Hard left. A fraction to the right. Then his foot went down, and
they were hurtling forward, passing the front of the car, but with
less than an inch to spare between the lorry on the left and the
rock face to the right.

Quite suddenly, they were through, back on the empty road
downhill into Monaco.

'Hoods?' He could feel Percy quivering beside him though her
voice betrayed no sign of fear.

'You mean our kind?'

She nodded, her mouth forming a small 'Yes.'

'Don't think so. Looked like a team out to take our money,
and anything else they could grab. There's always been plenty of
that along this coast. In the north of England they have a saying:
where there's muck there's brass. You can change that to where
there's money there's lice.'

Bond knew he was lying. It was just possible that the axemen
were a group of gangsters. But the set-up had been deadly in its
professionalism and sophistication. He would report it as soon as
he could get a safe line to London. He told Percy that he would
do just that.

'So shall I.'

They said nothing more until they got to her room. After that,
neither of them would ever be able to say what started it.

'They were pros,' she said.

'Yes.'

'I don't like it, James. I'm pretty experienced, but I can still get
frightened.'

She moved closer to him, and in a second his arms were
around her. Their lips met as though each was trying to breathe
fresh energy into the other. Her mouth slid away from him and
her cheek lay alongside his neck as she clung on, whispering his
name.

So they became lovers, their needs and feelings erupting,

adding urgency to every moment of the day and night. With this new mental and physical intermingling came a fresh anxiety, so that they worked harder than ever towards the final goal of preparing Bond to meet Percy's former husband.

By the start of the third week, as he was really beginning to master the intricacies of micro programs, Percy suddenly called a halt.

'I'm going to show you the kind of thing that Jay Autem could well be writing now,' she announced, switching off the Terror Twelve and removing the normal disk drives which Bond had just been using.

In their place she fitted a large, hard-disk laser drive and, powering up the system, booted a program into the computer – 'booting' being the technical term for placing a program in the computer's memory.

If Bond had found the computer TEWT fascinating, it was as child's play to the program he was about to witness. What appeared on the screen now was not the standard computer graphics he had become used to, even in their highest form, but genuine pictures, real and in natural colour and texture, like a controllable movie.

'Video,' Percy explained. 'A camera interfaced with a hard laser computer disk. Now watch.'

She manipulated the joystick, and it was as though they were driving along a city street in heavy traffic. Certainly the human forms she produced were less realistic than the background against which she made them move, run, fight and take action. But there was a new and almost frightening conviction about this presentation. It was more a simulation than a game.

'I call it Bank Robbery,' she said, and there was no doubt about its effectiveness. By the clever juxtaposition of real film and graphics you could play at robbing a real bank, dealing with every possible emergency that might arise. Bond was more than impressed.

'When I've taught you how to process and copy Jay Autem's work, you'll have the Terror Twelve and three types of drive to take with you, James. Don't say I haven't provided you with all the essential creature comforts.'

Until later that evening, Bond applied himself to the work, but remained introspective, his mind hovering between the tasks on hand and the appalling potential for evil of the tool that Jay Autem Holy – or indeed anyone with the necessary knowledge – had at his disposal.

It should have been obvious, of course. If there were programs to assist the military in learning strategy and tactics, there had to be the potential there for unscrupulous people to learn the best way to rob, cheat and even kill.

'And you really believe training programs, like the one you showed me today, are being used by criminals?' he asked much later, when they were in bed.

'I'd be very surprised if they weren't.' Percy's face was grave. 'Just as I'd be amazed if Jay Autem were not training criminals, or even terrorists, in his nice Oxfordshire house.' She gave a humourless little laugh. 'I doubt if it's called Endor by accident. The Holy Terror has a dark sense of humour.'

Bond knew that she was almost certainly right. Every two days he received a report from England, via Bill Tanner: a digest of the information coming from the surveillance team that had been set up with exceptional discretion, officers being changed every forty-eight hours, in the village of Nun's Cross. He asked Percy what she thought had actually happened on the night Dr Holy went missing.

'Well, he certainly didn't go by himself. Dear old Rolling Joe Zwingli must have gone with him, and that guy was as mad as a hatter. They had a file as long as your arm on him at Langley.'

'Dealt with the poor pilot, then jumped, I suppose?' Bond was almost speaking to himself.

Percy nodded, then shrugged. 'And did away with Zwingli when it suited him.'

During the final days of study, Bond mastered the art of copying all types of program protected by every method Percy knew to be used by Dr Holy. They saved the last two days for themselves.

'You're an enchantress,' Bond told Percy. 'I know of nobody else who could have taught me so much in such a short time.'

'You've given me a few wrinkles as well, and I don't mean on my face.' She put her head back on the pillow. 'Come on, James, darling, one more time, as the jazz men say, then we'll have a fabulous dinner and you can really show me how to play those tables in the Salles Privées.'

It was mid-afternoon, and by nine that evening they were seated at the first table in the Casino's most sacred of rooms. Bond's run of luck was still high, though he was now gambling with care, rarely going above his winning stake, which had quadrupled since his arrival, and not betting on the rash outside chance, high-win options.

During the three hours they played that night he was down, at one point, to 40,000 francs. But the wheel started to run in his favour, and eventually, by midnight, the stake had increased to 300,000 francs. He waited for two turns to pass, deciding to make the next bet the last of the night, when he heard a sharp intake of breath from Percy. Glancing towards her, he saw the colour had left her face, her eyes staring at the entrance. It was not so much a look of fear as of sudden surprise.

'What is it?'

She answered in a whisper, 'Let's get out. Quickly. Over there. Just come in . . .'

'Who?' Bond's eyes fell on a tall, grizzled man, straight-backed, and with eyes that swept the room as though surveying a battlefield. He did not really need to hear her reply.

'The old devil. And we thought Jay Autem had gone for him.

That's Rolling Joe in the flesh. Joe Zwingli's here, and with a couple of infantry divisions by the look of it!'

Zwingli was moving into the room, flanked by four other men, neat and smart as officers on parade, and looking as dangerous as an armoured brigade about to attack a Boy Scout troop.

7

ROLLING HOME

General Zwingli had been no chicken at the time of his disappearance. He must now be in his mid-seventies. Yet, from where Bond sat, he looked like a man of sixty in good physical shape. The four other men were younger, heavier and not the kind of people you would be likely to meet at Sunday school parties.

For a moment, Bond sat calmly awaiting the worst, convinced that Zwingli and his men were looking for him, or possibly Percy. There had to be a connection. You didn't need a crystal ball to work that out. Zwingli had been a necessary part of the disappearance plot. If there had been collusion at the time of the aeroplane wreck, there would still be collusion now, for Dr Holy and General Zwingli were tied together for life by a much stronger bond than marriage vows. Conspirators can rarely divorce without one partner seriously damaging the other.

Bond smiled genially. 'Don't stare, Percy. It's rude. It may also call the good General's attention to us – if it's us he's looking for.' His lips hardly moved as he watched Zwingli and his entourage out of the corner of his eye.

To his relief, the General's craggy face broke into a broad smile. He was not looking in Bond's and Percy's direction but advancing towards a dark-skinned muscular man, possibly in his mid-thirties, who had been sitting at the bar. The pair shook hands warmly, and there were greetings and introductions all round.

'I think, to be on the safe side, it would be prudent for us to take our leave now,' Bond muttered. 'Be casual and natural.'

He went through the business of tipping the croupier, gathering the chips together as they rose. They made their way to the *caisse*, where Bond opted for cash rather than a cheque. Once outside, he took Percy's arm, leading her firmly back to the hotel.

'It could simply be a coincidence, but I'm taking no chances. I don't for a moment think he could recognise you. How well did you know him, Percy?'

'Two or three dinner parties. Washington social functions. I knew him, but he always gave the impression of complete non-interest. Not just in me, but in all women. It was him all right, James. I've no doubt about that.'

During M's briefing Bond had studied a number of photographs, including two series in *Time* magazine, when General Zwingli had made the cover story. 'For someone who's been dead that long, he looked in exceptionally good shape. No, the only way he could recognise you is if he was forewarned: if he knew you'd changed your . . . well . . . your image.'

Percy giggled. 'This *is* my real image, James. Mrs Jay Autem Holy was the disguise. I put on weight, wore thick clear-glass spectacles and looked the ultimate frowsy computer scientist . . .'

'And the nose?'

'Okay, so I had it fixed after Jay Autem went missing. Nobody's perfect. But you're right, I'd have had to be fingered directly to Rolling Joe for him to know it was me . . .'

'There's always the possibility that someone's fingered *me*.' Bond brushed back the lock of hair which fell, like a comma, over his right eye. They reached the hotel entrance. 'You recognise the fellow he met? The swarthy man he seemed to be expecting?'

'The face was familiar. I've seen him before or a picture of him. Maybe he's on file. You?'

'Same here. I should know him.' Bond continued to talk, telling her they would have to leave Monte Carlo. 'It would be best for us both to get away in the Bentley. We can be in Paris by lunchtime tomorrow.'

'Wait until we're upstairs,' she mumbled. When they reached her room, Percy became adamant. 'My brief was to leave here on my own. I have a car, and orders that we go separately. Under no circumstances are we to travel together. Those are my instructions, and there's no way I'm going to disobey them.'

'So?'

'So I agree with you, James. I think it's merely a coincidence. It's also a useful piece of information, knowing that Zwingli is alive. And I think we should leave; the sooner, the better.'

For a while she fussed about Bond, like the proverbial mother hen, questioning him on all she had taught him.

He lugged the cases containing the Terror Twelve into his own room, together with the disk drives and utility programs on disks that would help him copy or recover Holy's listings, should he have the chance to get hold of any. Then they went their separate ways to pack, arranging to meet again for a quick farewell before Percy left a good half hour before Bond. They would both be taking roughly the same route, for Percy had to return to the CIA Paris Station, while Bond faced the long drive back to Calais and the ferry to Dover. They met as planned in the garage after Percy's luggage had been loaded into the boot of her sporty little blue Dodge 600ES.

'You think we'll ever meet again?' Bond felt uncharacteristically inadequate.

She put her hands on his shoulders, looking into the startling blue eyes. 'We have to, don't we, James?'

He nodded, knowing they shared each other's private thoughts. 'You know how to get in touch with me?'

It was her turn to give a small nod. 'Or you can call me – when all this is over.' She rattled off a Washington number. 'If I'm not there, they'll pass on a message, okay?'

Percy put her arms around his neck, kissing him, long and lovingly on the mouth. As she started up the Dodge, she leaned out of the window.

'Take care, James. I'll miss you.'

Then she was gone, in a smooth, controlled acceleration, along the lane of parked cars, up the ramp and into the streets of Monaco and the night roads of France.

Half an hour later, Bond took the Mulsanne Turbo out of the same garage. Within minutes he was out of the principality, heading back along the Moyenne Corniche on the road that would take him on to the main A8 Paris Autoroute.

It was on the first leg of the journey – at about four in the morning – that Bond suddenly remembered the identity of the man Zwingli had met. Yes, there *was* a file. The thick dossier had been across Bond's desk on many occasions, and there was a general watching brief on Tamil Rahani. Part American, part Lebanese, and carrying at least two passports, Rahani was usually based in New York, where he was chairman and principal share-holder of Rahani Electronics. He had made several attempts to secure defence contracts from both the American and British governments, mainly for aircraft communications electronics, though there had been some computerisation involved.

Rahani had first approached the Service some five years before, handed on to them by the American Service. They had turned him down flat because of his many contacts with unfriendly agencies and uncertain governments. He was wealthy, smooth, sharp, intelligent, and slippery as an eel. The flag on the file, Bond remembered, was ciphered *Possible clandestine. Probably subversive.*

Once these facts had settled in his mind, Bond pushed the Mulsanne to its limit. All he wanted to do was to get back to England, report to M, and try to move in on Jay Autem Holy. The task was more inviting than ever, now he knew both some-thing of the doctor's work, and the fact that Zwingli was alive, well, and – unless he was mistaken – working hand in glove with a highly suspect international character.

On the A26 Autoroute to Calais, Bond found himself singing aloud. Perhaps after the enforced idleness, the lack of excitement, the intrigues of M's plan to use him as bait, he was at last starting to feel the fire of action in his belly once more.

'Rolling home,' he sang, remembering far-off days when he would literally roll home, with brother officers,

'Rolling home,
By the light of the silvery moon;
I have twopence to lend,
And twopence to spend,
And twopence to send home to . . .'

His voice trailed off. He could not bring himself to sing the last line, about sending money home to his wife. For the ghost of his own dead wife, Tracy, still haunted him, even though he now missed Percy Proud's clear mind and agile, beautiful body. Weakness, he chided himself. He was trained as a loner, one who acted without others; one who relied on himself. Yet he did miss her. Undeniably, there were moments when he thought he could still smell her scent and feel the touch of her skin. Pull yourself together, he told himself.

Among the bills and circulars awaiting Bond at his flat was a letter from a firm of business consultants demanding special attention. Embedded in this seemingly innocous letter was a series of telephone numbers – one for each day of the week – that he could ring in order to set up a meeting with M at the safe flat near St Martin's Lane.

The date arranged turned out to be a truly glorious spring evening. Summer was around the corner, and you could almost feel it, even in the heart of the capital.

'Well, 007, the woman's taught you all the tricks of the trade, eh?'

'Some of them, sir. But I really wanted to talk to you about a new development.'

Without wasting words or time, he gave a summary of the final hours in Monaco, and the sighting of Zwingli with Tamil Rahani. Bond had hardly got Rahani's name out before M ordered the Chief-of-Staff to check.

'There's a spot and report order on that joker.'

Tanner returned in ten minutes. 'Last report of a visit to Milan. Seen by our resident there, who had a weather eye on him. Rahani appeared to be on his usual round of business meetings.' The Chief-of-Staff gave a somewhat dejected shrug. 'Unhappily, sir, nobody spotted him leaving, though his airline ticket showed a return booking to New York yesterday. He was not on the flight.'

'And I suppose nobody's seen hide nor hair of him since.' M nodded in reply like a buddha. 'Except 007, in Monaco.'

'Well, he was in the Casino,' said Bond, 'with General Zwingli and four others.'

M looked at him in silence for a long time. 'Incredible,' he said at last, as though someone had hit him in the face. 'Incredible that Zwingli's still alive, let alone mixed up with Rahani. Wonder where he fits into all this. You'll just have to be alert to Rahani's possible involvement, 007. He's always been a bit of an unknown quantity, so we'll inform those who need to know. You see, we're ready to put you in. Now, here's what I want you to do. First, your old acquaintance Freddie Fortune has . . .'

James Bond groaned loudly.

For the next week, he was to be seen around his old London haunts. He confided in one or two people that his feelings of disillusion had become considerably worse. He had been in Monte Carlo where things had run true to the old adage: lucky at cards, unlucky in love – except it had been roulette, not cards.

Carefully, he laid a trail among people most likely to talk, or those whose connections were right for some salting. Then, on the Thursday evening, in the bar of one of Mayfair's plush clubs, as if by accident, he bumped into Lady Freddie Fortune, the extravagant, pamphlet-wagging socialite he always called his 'champagne communist'. She was a vivacious, petite redhead, 'Red Freddie', some called her – completely untrustworthy, and always in the gossip columns, either campaigning for some outrageous cause or involved in sexual scandal. Freddie was discreet only when it suited her. That night, Bond dropped a hint that he was looking for work in the computer field. He also poured out all his troubles – an affair in Monte Carlo that had ended disastrously, leaving him bitter and wretched.

Lady Freddie was thrilled to see this man, once a model of good form, become so emotional and she whipped Bond off to her bed, allowing him to cry on her shoulder – metaphorically, of course. During the night, trying to keep up the pretence of having drunk too much yet still able to enjoy himself, Bond longed for Percy and the special smell and feel of her.

The next morning he feigned a hangover and morose, even waspish, manner. But none of this put Freddie Fortune off. As he was leaving she told him that she had some friends who may be of use to him, if he really meant to find a job in computer programming.

'Here.' She tucked a small business card into his breast pocket. 'It's a nice little hotel. If you can make it on Saturday, I'll be there. Only, for heaven's sake, don't let on I've told you. I leave it to you, James, but if you do decide to come, be surprised to see me. Okay?'

On the following Saturday morning, with a weekend case and all the computer equipment in the boot, James Bond drove the Bentley out of London on the Oxford road. Within the hour he had turned off and was threading through country lanes on his way to the village of Nun's Cross, near Banbury.

8

THE BULL

Banbury Cross is not an antiquity, but was erected in the late 1850s to commemorate the marriage of the Princess Royal to the Crown Prince of Prussia. There was of course a much earlier cross – three to be exact – but the present Victorian Gothic monstrosity was placed where it is today because a local historian believed this to be the site of the ancient High Cross. Three miles to the north of Banbury, nestling by a wooded hill, lies the village of Nun's Cross, and there is no cross on view there at all.

Bond guided the Mulsanne Turbo through the narrow main street of Nun's Cross, and into the yard of the coaching inn which rejoices in the name of The Bull at the Cross. Taking his overnight case from the boot, he considered the inn was probably the only going concern in the village. A beautiful Georgian building, lovingly kept, and neatly modernised, The Bull even offered 'gourmet weekends for the discriminating'.

From the porter who took his case, Bond learned that, as far as the hotel was concerned, it was going to be a very quiet weekend, though they had been full the previous one.

Bond unpacked, changed into grey slacks, an open-necked shirt topped by a navy pullover and his most comfortable moccasins. He was not armed. The ASP 9mm lay comfortably clipped into its hidden compartment in the Bentley. Yet he remained alert as he went down, through the old coach yard and into the village street. His eyes were searching for a dark blue Jaguar XJ6 or a grey Mercedes-Benz saloon. The licence numbers had been committed to memory, for both cars had appeared in his mirror, exchanging places with monotonous regularity ever since he had taken to the road that morning.

He was under no illusion. For the first time since he had assumed the mantle of a disaffected former member of the Secret Service, he was being followed, almost blatantly, as though the tail wished to be seen.

It was too early for a lunchtime drink. Bond decided to look round this village which, if everything added up, harboured a sophisticated villain who was possibly also a traitor.

The Bull at the Cross lay almost on the crossroads at the centre of the old village, which contained a hodgepodge of mainly Georgian buildings, with a sprinkle of slightly older terraced houses that were now the village shops, leaning in on one another as though mutually dependant. Small rows of what must at one time have been labourers' cottages now housed people who commuted into Banbury or Oxford, to labour in different fields.

Almost opposite the coach yard entrance stood the church. To the south, the main street meandered out into open country, scattered with copses and studded with larger houses, as though the more prosperous local gentry had landscaped the southern vista with their properties. Gateways and rhododendron-flanked drives gave glimpses of large, sedate Victorian mansions or glowing Hornton stone Georgian buildings.

The third driveway past the church was walled, with heavy, high modern gates set into the original eighteenth-century stone. A small brass plate engraved with the words GUNFIRE SIMULATIONS LTD was sunk into the pillar to the right of the gates. In newer stone, carved and neatly blended with the original, was the one word, ENDOR.

The drive, which turned abruptly, disappearing behind thick low trees and bushes, seemed to be neatly kept, and a strip of grey slate was only just visible some two hundred yards in the distance. Bond calculated the size of the grounds to be about a square mile. The high wall continued to his left, the boundary being a narrow dirt track neatly signposted THE SHRUBS.

After half a mile or so he turned back along the village street and on towards the northern extremity, where the cluster of old houses bordered a scrubby, wooded hill. Here sharp speculators had been at work, and a modern housing estate encroached almost on the woodland itself.

It was gone twelve when Bond ambled slowly back to the inn. A dark blue Jaguar stood not far from the Bentley but no one except the staff appeared to be about. In the private bar he found only the barman and one other guest.

'James, darling, what a surprise to find *you* here, out in the sticks!' Freddie Fortune, neat in an emerald shirt and tight jeans sat in a window seat.

'The surprise is mutual, Freddie. Drinking?'

'Vodka and tonic, darling.'

He got the drinks from a friendly barman, and carried them over to Freddie, saying loudly, 'What brings you here, then?'

'Oh, I adore this place. I often come down to commune with nature – and friends. Not your sort of place though, James.' Then quietly, 'So glad you could make it.'

Bond said he was glad too. 'On a bit of a downer. Sorry about the other night, Freddie. Must've bored the pants off you . . .'

'Oh no, darling, I wouldn't say that,' she murmured. 'It was frightfully touching, actually. I felt terribly sorry for you, poor lamb.'

'Made an ass of myself. Forget what I said, eh?' Bond felt unutterably foolish, putting on the style of Freddie's London friends.

'Forgotten already, darling.' She took a quick sip of her vodka and tonic. 'So you wanted to get out of the hurly-burly, yah?'

'Yah.' Bond almost mimicked her affected accent.

'Or did you come because *I* asked you?'

He gave a non-committal 'Mmmm.'

'Or, perhaps, the possibility of work?'

'Little of all three, Freddie.'

'Three's a crowd.' She snuggled up beside him. For a second, Bond felt, strangely, that Percy was there.

They lunched together from a menu that would not have put the Connaught to shame, then walked for five miles or so across the fields and through the woodland, getting back around three-thirty.

'Just in time for a nice quiet siesta.'

Freddie gave him the come-to-bed look, and Bond, invigorated by the walk, was in no mood to disappoint. First, though, he made an excuse to go over to the Bentley, where he retrieved the ASP 9mm and two spare clips of ammunition, keeping them well hidden when he joined Freddie in the comfort of her room.

She was lying on the bed, wearing precious little. Smiling sweetly, she said, 'Come and bore the pants off me, darling.'

'Dinner?' Bond asked later, as they sat over tea in the residents' lounge. The hotel had filled up, and three Spanish waiters scurried about with silver teapots, small plates of sandwiches and fancy cakes. Like Brown's on Sunday afternoon, but without the polish, Bond thought.

'Oh lord, darling.' Freddie put on her 'devastated' face. 'I have a dinner date.' Then she smiled. 'So have you, if we play our cards right. You see, I've got some old friends who live here.' She suddenly became confidential. 'Now listen, James, they could be a godsend. You were serious about going into computers? Programming and all that sort of thing? Micros?'

'Absolutely.'

'Super. Old Jason'll be thrilled.'

'Jason?'

'My friend – well friends, really. Jason and Dazzle St John-Finnes.'

'Dazzle?'

Freddie gave an impatient back-flip of her hand – 'Oh, her name's Davide or something. Everyone calls her Dazzle. Super people. Into computers in a really big way. They're incredibly clever and invent frightfully complicated war games.'

M had already briefed him about the other members of Jay Autem Holy's entourage: the 'wife', Dazzle; a young expert called Peter Amadeus ('Austrian, I think,' Freddie now added); and the even younger Cambridge graduate, Cindy Chalmer.

'She's an absolute hoot.' Freddie became expansive. 'The locals call her Sinful Cindy, and she's jolly popular, particularly with the men. Black, you know.'

No, Bond said, he did not know. But he would like to find out. How did Sinful Cindy get on with Peter Amadeus?

'Oh, darling, no woman has anything to fear – or hope for – from the Amadeus boy, if you see what I mean. Look, I'll give Jason a bell.' Freddie, like many of her kind, affected the London vernacular, particularly when out of town. Just to make certain they don't mind me having you in tow.'

She disappeared for about five minutes, though Bond already knew what the answer would be. Freddie, he had to admit, was a nice little actress.

'We've got a result, James,' she said when she came back. 'They'd absolutely adore to have you to dinner.' Just as he knew they would, and she knew they would.

In spite of her affected accent, rather silly manner, and undeniable sexual availability, Freddie Fortune was a loyal friend, naïve in her judgments, but, once committed, to cause or person, she became unshakeable. Almost certainly, in this instance, Freddie was being used, Bond thought. She probably did not even begin to understand the risks or dangers which could face him, and possibly herself.

Gently he questioned her in an attempt to discover how long 'Old Jason and Dazzle' had been such close friends. She hedged a little, but it finally transpired that she had known them for exactly two months.

They went in the Bentley.

'I adore the smell of leather in a car. So positively sexual.'

Freddie curled up in the large armchair-sized front passenger seat. Bond was careful to ask for directions.

'The gates will probably be closed, but turn in and wait. Jason's a maniac about security. He has lots of incredible electronic devices.'

'I'll bet,' Bond said under his breath, but obeyed instructions, turning left where she told him and pushing the Mulsanne's snout to within an inch of the great high metal barriers. He would have put money on their being made of steel, worked to give the impression of ornamental wrought iron. There were three great locks – and the gate-hangings were shielded behind massive stone pillars.

There had to be some kind of closed-circuit television system, for the car sat waiting only a matter of seconds before the locks clicked audibly and the gates swung back.

As Bond had already divined, Endor was a large house with about twenty rooms: classical Georgian in golden Cotswold stone, with a pillared porch and symmetrically placed sash windows. The crunch of gravel under the Bentley's wheels was a sound that brought back many memories to him – the older cars he had once owned, and, oddly, school days when he read the books of Dornford Yates, with their adventurers riding forth to do battle in Bentleys or Rolls-Royce cars, usually to protect gorgeous ladies with very small feet.

Jason St John-Finnes – Bond had to think of him by that name – stood by the open door, light shafting on to the turning circle. He had made no attempt at disguise. The decade in which he had been 'dead' appeared to have taken no toll, for he looked exactly like the many photographs in his file at the Regent's Park Headquarters. Tall and slim, he was obviously in good physical condition, for he moved with grace and purpose – an athlete's walk. The famous green eyes were just as startling as everyone maintained. By turns warm or cold, they were almost hypnotic, lively and penetrating, as though they could look deeply into a person's heart. The nose was indeed large and hooked, a great bill, so that the combination of bright searching eyes and the big sharp nose certainly gave the impression of a bird of prey. Bond shuddered inwardly. There was something exceptionally sinister about Dr Jay Autem Holy. Yet this unsettling fact vanished the moment he started to speak.

'Freddie!' He approached her with a kiss. 'How splendid to see you, and I'm so glad to meet your friend.' He stretched out a hand. 'Bond, isn't it?'

The voice was low, pleasant, and full of laughter, the accent mid-Atlantic, almost Bostonian, the handshake firm, strong, warm and very friendly. It was as though a wave of goodwill and welcome were transmitted when their palms touched.

'Ah, here's Dazzle. Darling, this is Mr Bond.'

'James,' he said, already in danger of being hypnotically charmed by the man. 'James Bond.'

For a few seconds his heart raced as he gazed at the tall, slim ash-blonde woman who had come out of the house. Then he realised that it was a trick of the light; but at a distance, especially as now at dusk, Dazzle could easily be taken for Percy Proud: the same hair, figure and bone structure, even the same movements.

Dazzle was as warm and welcoming as her husband. The pair had a curious effect, as though together they were able to enfold you, pulling you into some circle of enchantment. As they left the car and walked into the spacious hallway, Bond had a ridiculous desire to throw all caution to the wind, sit down and face Jason immediately, asking him what really happened on that day so long ago when he had taken off on the ill-fated flight. What was the purpose of disappearing? What was he up to now? And how did Zwingli fit into the scheme of things?

That evening, Bond had to keep a strong hold on himself not to come out into the open. Between them Jason and the vivacious Dazzle proved to be a daunting couple. Within minutes of being in their company you became almost old friends. Jason, the story went, was Canadian by birth, while Dazzle was from

New York, though you would have been hard put to it to place her accent, which had more of Knightsbridge than Fifth Avenue in it.

The one subject never discussed in detail during M's briefings had been finance, but now, seeing the house with its discreetly elegant decor ('That's Dazzle,' Jason said with a laugh, 'she has what the designers call flair') made one aware of great riches. In the large drawing room there was a clever blend of original Georgian and comfortable modern, the antique pieces complemented by a quiet, striped wallpaper, and not clashing with the more modern pictures or the deep, comfortable armchairs and sofas. Where, Bond wondered, did the money for all this come from? Could Gunfire Simulations finance so much?

While a Filipino houseboy served the drinks the talk was almost exclusively about what a wonderful refurbishing job they had done on the house, and the local amusing scandal.

'It's what I adore about life in a village.' Jason gave a low chuckle. 'My work doesn't allow me to be what you might call socially active, but we still get all the gossip – because everybody does.'

'Except the gossip about ourselves, darling,' Dazzle said with a grin. Bond realised that her nose was similar to Percy's before it had been bobbed. Here was an oddity. She really was like the true Percy. Did Jay Autem know, he wondered. Had he always known what the real Percy looked like? Had he seen her since the recent transformation?

'Oh, I get the gossip about us.' Jason's voice was deep with humour. 'Cindy and I are having a passionate love affair, while you're in bed most of the time with Felix . . .'

'Much good would it do me!' Dazzle put a hand over her mouth, mockingly. 'Where are they, anyway, dear? Peter and Cindy, I mean.'

'Oh, they'll be up in a minute. They decided to play one more round of The Revolution. We've still got a good deal of preliminary work to do.' He turned to Bond. 'We're in the computer games business . . .'

'So Freddie mentioned.' At last he managed to break the spell, allowing a hint of superior disapproval into his tone.

Jason caught it at once. 'Oh, but you're a computer programmer as well, aren't you? Freddie told me.'

'A little. Not games though. Not really.' The tiny stress on the word *games* was calculated to give the impression that using computers to play games was anathema to him.

'Aha.' Jason wagged a finger. 'But there are games and games, Mr Bond. I'm talking about complex intellectual simulations, not the whizz-bang-shoot-'em-up arcade rubbish. For whom do you work?'

Bond admitted he worked for nobody at the moment. 'I had my training in programming when I worked for the Foreign Office.' He tried to sound diffident.

'You're *that* Mr Bond!' Dazzle sounded genuinely excited.

He nodded. 'Yes, the notorious Mr Bond. Also, the innocent Mr Bond.'

'Of course. I read about your case.' For the first time there was a slightly dubious note in Jason's voice.

'Were you really a spy?' Dazzle tended to become almost breathlessly excited by anything that interested her.

'I . . .' Bond began, then put on a show of floundering, so that Jason came to his rescue: 'I don't think that's the kind of question you're meant to ask, my dear.' At that moment, Peter Amadeus and Cindy Chalmer came into the room.

'Ah, the amazing Doctor Amadeus.' Jason rose.

'And Sinful Cindy,' said Dazzle with a laugh.

'I'd be flattered if they called *me* Sinful Freddie,' said Lady Freddie as she greeted the pair.

'Sinful indeed!' Cindy was not black, as Freddie had told Bond, but more of a creamy coffee shade. 'The product of a West Indian father and a Jewish mother,' she was later to confide in him, adding that there were a thousand racist jokes which could be made at her expense. Now she just repeated, 'Sinful indeed; chance would be more than a fine thing.'

Dressed in a simple grey skirt, and white silk blouse, Cindy had the figure and legs of a dancer, and a face which reminded Bond of a very young Ella Fitzgerald.

Peter was around thirty – a few years older than Cindy. Slightly built, immaculately dressed and prematurely balding, he had a precise pedantry and wit that gave a hint of his sexual predeliction. Following Cindy's remark, he helped himself to a drink, saying, 'You've got plenty of chances here, Cindy. There are some great big farm boys in the village I'd fight you for . . .'

'That's enough, Peter!' For the first time that night, Jason showed the steel fist.

After the introductions (Bond wondered if he imagined it, but Cindy Chalmer appeared to give him a sharp, almost conspiratorial look when they shook hands), Dazzle suggested they go in to dinner. 'Tomas will be furious if his cooking is spoiled.' Tomas was the silent Filipino, who had learned to cook at the feet of Europe's greatest chefs, by courtesy of Jason St John-Finnes.

The meal was almost a banquet: a Lombardy soup of hot consommé poured over raw eggs sprinkled with Parmesan and laid on lightly fried bread; smoked salmon mousse; venison marinated and roasted with juniper berries, wine, chopped ham and lemons: and a soufflé au Grand Marnier – 'Specially for Lady Freddie.'

To begin with, the conversation mainly concerned the work Cindy and Peter had just been doing.

'How did it go, then?' Jason asked as they sat down, at a long refectory table set on bare polished boards in the dining room.

'We've found two more random problems you can set into the early section. Raise the general and search strengths of the British patrols, and you get some very interesting results.' Peter gave a lopsided smile.

'And, to equalise, there's a new random for the later stages,'

Cindy added. 'We've put in a random card that gives the Colonial Militia more uncaptured cannon. If you draw that option the British don't know the strength until they begin assaulting the hill.'

Freddie and Dazzle were chattering away about clothes, but Jason caught Bond's interested eye. He turned to Peter and Cindy.

'Mr Bond doesn't approve of using such high-tech magic for mere games.' He smiled, the comment bearing no malice.

'Ah, come on, Mr Bond!'

'It's intellectual stimulation.'

Cindy and Peter leapt to Holy's defence simultaneously. Peter continued, 'Is chess a frivolous use of wood or ivory?'

'I said nothing of the kind,' said Bond, laughing. He knew that the testing time was getting close. 'I was simply trained as a programmer in Cobol, databases and the use of graphics – for government purposes . . .'

'Not military purposes, Mr Bond?'

'Oh, the military use them, of course. When I was a naval officer we didn't have the benefit of that kind of technology.' He paused. 'I would in fact be intrigued to hear about your work. These games – are they really games?'

'They are games in one sense,' Peter answered. 'I suppose they're also tutorials. A lot of serving military people order our products.'

'They teach, yes.' Jason leaned over towards Bond. 'You cannot sit down and play one of our games unless you have some knowledge of strategy, tactics and military history. They can be taxing, and they do require intelligence. It's a booming market, James.' He paused, as though a thought had struck him. 'What's the most significant leap forward in the computer arts – in your opinion, of course?'

Bond did not hesitate. 'Oh, without doubt the advances being made, almost by the month, in vastly increased storage of data using smaller and smaller space.'

Jason nodded. 'Yes. Increased memory in decreased space. Millions of accessible facts, stored for all time in something no larger than a postage stamp. And, as you say, it's advancing by the month, even by the day. In a year or so, the little home micro will be able to store almost as much information as the large mainframe computers used by banks and government departments. There is also the breakthrough that marries the laser video disk recording with computer commands – movements, actions, scale, response. At Endor we have a very sophisticated set-up. You may like to look around after dinner.'

'Put him on The Revolution and see if a novice player comes up with anything new,' suggested Cindy.

'Why not?' The bright green eyes glittered, as though some challenge were in the offing.

'You've made a computer game out of what? The Russian Revolution?'

Jason laughed. 'Not quite, James. You see, our games are vast, in a way too large for the home computer. They're all very detailed and need a big memory. We pride ourselves on their playability as well as their high level of intellectual stimulation. In fact, we don't like calling them games. Simulations is a better word.

'No, we haven't yet got a simulation of any revolution. At the moment, we have only six on the market: Crécy, Blenheim, the Battle of the Pyramids – Napoleon's Egyptian expedition – Austerlitz, Cambrai, which is very good, because the outcome could have been very different; and Stalingrad. We're also very well advanced with one on the Blitzkrieg of 1940. And we are preparing an interesting one on the American Revolution – you know, the final stages prior to the War of Independence: Concord, Lexington, Bunker's Hill. September 1774 to June 1775.'

'Freddie and I are going to look at the conservatory,' Dazzle suddenly interrupted, rather sharply. 'It's shop all the time. Very boring. Hope to see you later, James. Lovely meeting you.'

Jason did not even apologise, merely smiling benignly and

shrugging. Freddie gave Bond a broad wink as the two ladies left the room. As he turned back to the table, he caught Cindy looking at him again, in the same almost conspiratorial way, tinged this time with jealousy. Or did he imagine it?

Jason had hardly paused. 'Naturally, you're conversant with flowcharting a computer program, James?'

Bond nodded, recalling the hours spent in Monaco drawing the complex charts which showed exactly what you wanted the computer to do. Once more, with the memory came that odd sense of Percy's presence. He dragged himself back, for Jason was still speaking.

'Before we prepare a detailed flowchart, we have to find out what we want to chart. So we begin to plan the simulation by playing it on a large table. This acts as our graphics guide, and we have counters for units, troops, ships, cannon, plus cards for the random possibilities: weather cards, epidemics, unexpected gains or losses, hazards of war.'

Peter took over. 'From this we learn the scope of the program task. So, when we've played the campaign . . .'

'About a million times,' Cindy added. 'It seems like a million, anyway.'

Peter nodded '. . . We're ready to begin flowcharting the various sections. You have to be dedicated in this job.'

'Come down to the laboratory.' Jason's voice became commanding. 'We'll show James the board we're working on now. Who knows, he may get interested and return to battle it out with me. If you do,' he said, looking intently at Bond, 'make sure you have plenty of time. Campaigns cannot be fought in five minutes.'

Behind these seemingly pleasant words there was a hint of obsession that Bond found disturbing.

As they left the room, he was conscious of Cindy brushing against him. He felt her hand touch his right hip lightly, just where the ASP 9mm was holstered. Had that been accidental, or was she carrying out a subtle search? Whatever the answer, Cindy Chalmer, at least, knew that he was armed.

They went through the main hall, where Jason produced a bunch of keys attached to a thin gold chain, unlocking a door which, he said, had once been the way down to the cellars.

'We've made a few changes, naturally.'

'Naturally,' responded Bond, unprepared for the nature of the alterations. Below the house there were three large, well-equipped, computer rooms, with models of all the best-known micros sitting in front of their visual display units. In a fourth room, Jason's office, Bond's heart leapt as he spotted a machine that looked almost exactly like the Terror Twelve now safe outside in the Bentley's boot.

From his office Jason led the way into a long chamber, lit from above by at least thirty spotlights. The walls were covered with charts and maps and in the centre was a large table. Almost entirely covering the table and overlaid with a thick plastic grid was a detailed map of the eastern seaboard of America, centred on Boston as it was in the 1770s. The main communicating roads and natural features were clearly marked in colour. In the centre of the grid stood a rectangular framework made of black plastic, the size and shape of a large television screen, while two small easels had been placed at the far end. Two trays, on opposite sides of the table, contained packs of white three-by-five cards. There was a chair in front of each tray and a desk top to each player's right, well-stocked with paper, maps and printed forms.

Peter and Cindy began to explain the nature of the game, and how it was used to build up all the details of the simulation before anything was committed to a computer program. The black plastic frame moved both vertically and horizontally across the map.

'That is the area a player will eventually see on his screen, when we have built the game,' said Jason. His manner had become less warm, as though the professional had suddenly ousted the friendly side of his nature. He explained how they could slot close-ups of the terrain into the rectangle. 'When we've got the game on computer, you'll be able to scroll around this whole map, but see only one section at a time,' he said. 'However, there's a zoom facility. You press the Z key, and the screen will give you a blow-up of the section you've moved to.'

Cindy explained that the two easels contained a calendar and the weather cards; each month's cards were shuffled separately before play began. 'Weather restricts or enhances movement.' She demonstrated how the British patrols could move five spaces, on good days, but in heavy rain only three, and in snow, two.

Looking at the map, Bond tried to remember the history of that period, learned too long ago now in dusty schoolrooms. He thought of the frustration among officers of the Colonial Militia, of the British inability to protect the cities and towns, of the unrest, then rebellion and open hostility.

Then there was a general (was it General Gage?) caught between his situation on the ground and having to await orders from England. There were the patrols searching for the rebels' arms caches, Paul Revere's warning ride and the militia's weapons being moved out of Concord; then the skirmishes around that town and Lexington. The British had withdrawn into Boston and fought at Bunker's Hill, remembered as a kind of Dunkirk by the Americans, for the British garrison had won the battle, but with such terrible losses that they had to retreat by sea to Halifax.

Bond thought of these things as Jason, warming to his theme, explained the way the simulation was played, with the players taking turns to issue orders and move forces. Some of the moves could be secret, and had to be noted on paper. Later came challenging and, possibly, skirmishing.

'The thing I find interesting is that you can alter history. I am, personally, very attached to the idea of changing history.' Again, a hint of that obsession, verging on dangerous madness.

'Perhaps I shall alter history,' Jason went on in a menacing whisper. 'A dream? Maybe, but dreams can turn into reality if one man with a brilliant mind is put to proper use. You think my spark of genius is put to proper use? No?' He expected no answer, and his next words really concerned something far beyond the simulation. 'Perhaps, James, we could look at this in more detail – even play a few rounds – say, tomorrow?'

Bond said he would like that, sensing more than an ordinary challenge. St John-Finnes continued to talk of revolution, change, and the complexity of war games. Cindy made an excuse to leave, nodding at Bond and remarking that she hoped they would meet again.

'Oh, I'm certain you will.' Jason appeared to be very sure of himself. 'I'm inviting James to have another look. Shall we say six tomorrow evening?'

Bond accepted, noticing that Jason did not even smile.

As they left, Jason walked on ahead, but Peter lingered to the rear with Bond, taking the opportunity to whisper, 'If you do play with him, he likes to win. Bad loser, and plays according to history. He always thinks his opponent will re-enact the actual events. The man's a paradox.' He gave Bond a wink, making it all too clear that Peter Amadeus was not particularly fond of his boss.

Upstairs, Dazzle awaited them, having driven Freddie back to the Bull. 'She seemed very tired. Said you had dragged her all round the countryside this afternoon, Mr Bond. You really shouldn't subject her to so much physical exercise. She's very much a town mouse, you know.'

Bond had his own thoughts about this. He too could do with a good night's sleep, but accepted the offer of a nightcap from his host. Cindy had gone to bed and Peter and Dazzle made their excuses, leaving the two men alone.

After a short silence, Jason raised his glass. 'Tomorrow,' he said, the green eyes like glass. 'Maybe we won't play games, James. But, I would welcome the chance of taking you on. Who knows? Computers, yes . . .' He was away again, in some world of his own with a different time, place and set of values. 'Computers are either the greatest tool mankind has invented, the most magnificent magic, capable of the construction of a new age,' he laughed, one sharp rising note, 'or they're the best toy God has provided.' In a couple of seconds the more familiar, benign Jason seemed to return. 'Can I share my thoughts about you, James? I think . . .' Jason was not waiting for Bond's reply or consent, 'I think that you are a small fraud, Mr Bond. That you know very little about the art of computer programming. Some, but not as much as you pretend. Am I right?'

'No.' Bond was firm. 'No, you're not right, I've taken the standard courses they give people like me. I reckon that I'm adequate. Not in your class, maybe, but who is?'

'Plenty of people.' Jason's voice was quiet. 'Young Cindy, and Peter, to name two. It's a young people's profession, and future, James. Yes, I have a lot of knowledge, and some flair for strategy. But young people who are brought up with the machines acquire flair very quickly. You know the age of the biggest, richest software tycoon in the United States?'

'Twenty-eight.'

'Right. Twenty-eight years old, and some of the really advanced programmers are younger. I know it all, but it's up to people like Cindy or Peter, to translate my ideas into reality. Brilliance, genius, requires nurturing. Programmers like my two may not really understand that they feed my great conceptions. As for you, a man with minimal training – you cannot be of real use to me. You don't stand a chance in this field.'

Bond shrugged. 'Not against you,' he said, not knowing whether this was some devious wordplay, some psychological ploy.

At the door, Jason told him he looked forward to the next meeting. 'If you feel you can take me on – at a game I mean – I'll be happy to oblige. But maybe we'll find something more interesting than games, eh? Six tomorrow.'

Bond could not know that the game of life itself would have changed by the time he saw Jay Autem Holy again. Nor what was really at stake in the games this curiously changeable man liked to play. He did know that Holy was a man possessed. Beneath the bonhomie and charm lay the mind of one who would play God with the world, and he found this deeply disturbing.

When he got back to the hotel, Bond retrieved his key from a dozing night porter and went up to his room. But, on putting the key in the lock, he found the door already open. Freddie, he thought, with some irritation, for he wanted very much to be alone, to have time to think.

Remaining cautious, he slipped the automatic pistol from its holster, and holding it just behind his right thigh, he turned the handle and gently kicked the door open.

'Hallo, Mr Bond.' Cindy Chalmer smiled up at him from one of the chairs, her long legs sprawled out in front of her, like an invitation.

Quietly, Bond closed the door.

'I bring greetings from Percy.' Cindy's smile broadened into a bewitching grin.

Bond remembered the looks she had given him during the evening. 'Who's Percy?' he asked evenly, holding her eyes in his, trying to detect either truth or deception.

9

INSIDE ENDOR

'Come on, Mr Bond. Percy Proud. Persephone. We're in ca-hoots.'

'Sorry, Cindy. Nice of you to drop by, but I've never heard of Percy, Persephone, or Proud.'

He quietly slipped the automatic pistol back into its holster. Cindy would have to do better than this if he was going to accept her. Face value and a mention of Percy was not enough.

We've even infiltrated Endor, he heard Percy whisper into the echo-chamber of his mind.

'You're very good.' Cindy spoke like a cheeky schoolgirl. 'Percy said you were. She also told me that I had to mention you liked treats, and an apple for the teacher always brought great rewards.'

Bond wasn't convinced yet. Certainly only Percy and he knew of his by-play with the apple in Monte Carlo and their jokes about rewards for pupils. But what if Percy's cover had been blown?

'You're in cahoots – as you put it – with someone called Percy?' he said, staring her out.

Cindy bobbed her head. 'Cahoots, intrigue, in league with. We both belong to the same outfit, Mr Bond.'

It made some sense. If the American Service already had some-one in the house, close to Jay Autem Holy, they would not broadcast the fact. Persephone, as a true professional, would not tell Bond either. The circle of people who knew would be confined until the last minute. So, was this the last minute?

'Tell me more.'

'She said – Percy said – you'd know what to do with these.' Cindy produced two hard disks encased in plastic from her shoulder bag. The thin boxes measured about five inches square and less than a quarter of an inch deep. On one side they had a hinged flap, like those on much fatter video cassettes. The boxes were brilliant blue and had small labels stuck on one corner.

Bond made no move even to touch them. 'And what, Miss Chalmer, are those?'

'A couple of our target's less conventional programs. And I can't hang on to them for long. At about four in the morning I turn into a pumpkin.'

'I'll get a couple of white mice to drive you home then.'

'Seriously. I can manage to get past the security without being detected until about four. They change shifts then.'

'We're talking of getting back into Endor I take it?'

'Of course we're talking about Endor. The place is electronically buttoned like Fort Knox – you remember Fort Knox?' Cindy gave a small, almost mocking smile. 'Well, Endor has code and lock combinations which change with each security shift. I have to go back during the current phase, otherwise I shall be right up the proverbial creek without a paddle.'

Bond asked if she did this often.

'In the mating season, yes. That's why I've cultivated a certain reputation in the village. So I have a kind of alibi if I ever get caught. But, if they cop me with these stuffed down my shirt . . . Well . . .' She ran a finger over her throat. 'So, Mr Bond, I'd appreciate it if you'd copy these little beauties.'

'How unconventional are they?' He reached out to take the disks, feeling as though something irrevocable would happen once he laid hands on them. Even to handle the things implied that he *could* do as Cindy asked. If this was an attempt to put him in the frame, there could be no going back.

'You'll see. But please do what has to be done as quickly as you can. I have no way of copying them at the house . . .'

'You can borrow them but not take copies? I find that difficult to believe, Miss Chalmer. Your boss told me, not long ago, that you're a wizard with these things.'

She made an irritated, spluttering noise which reminded him of M when the Head of Service became annoyed. 'Technically, of course I can copy. But it would be far too dangerous to try it in the house. I'm never left alone long enough with the hardware. Either the great man's around, or the Queen of the Night is fussing about . . .'

'The who?'

'Queen of . . . Oh, Peter. That's my pet name for him. I think he may well be trustworthy – he certainly loathes the boss – but it's not worth the risk. Percy wouldn't hear of it.'

Bond smiled inwardly. 'Cindy?'

She raised her eyes, ready for any question.

'How well do you know this Percy?'

'You're dreadfully coy, James.' They now slipped easily into first name terms.

'No, I'm just dreadfully careful.'

'I know her quite well. Have done for the past . . . what? Eight years?'

'Has she been hospitalised since you've known her? Medical operations of any kind?'

'A nose job. Spectacular. That's all.'

'And you?'

'I've never had one.'

'Background, Cindy. What? Who? And why?'

'All of it? Okay. I spent eight months in a hospital for infectious diseases after I left high school. There are medical records, doctors and nurses who remember me. I know because Old Bald Eagle's ferrets checked them out. Only I wasn't there. I was at the Farm, being trained. Then, surprise, I won a scholarship to Cambridge, here in England. From then on, as pure as the

driven. A good, hard-working girl. I'm untouchable, fully sani-
tised, as we say. The Company kept me on ice. I worked for IBM,
and then with Apple, before I applied for the job with Jay Autem
Holy. His boys checked, double-checked and even then didn't
trust me for eighteen months.'

Bond gave a brisk nod. There were no real options left. Trust
between him and the girl had to be entered into quickly, though
not lightly. 'Okay, just tell me about these two programs.'

'Why don't you take a look for yourself? Percy told me you
had the means.'

'You tell me, Cindy. Concisely as you can, then we'll get on
with it.'

She talked rapidly, reducing the information, telescoping her
sentences to the minimum. They had games weekends at Endor
– he knew about that – and some very strange people turned up
along with the usual, dedicated war games freaks.

'There are two particular characters – Balmer and Hopcraft,'
Cindy went on after pausing to gaze intently into Bond's eyes,
'known to my crowd as Tigerbalm and Happy. Tigerbalm's about
as balmy as a force ten blizzard. Kill you quick as look at you; and
Happy's probably only that way when he's raping or pillaging.
Happy would have made a good Viking raider.'

Cindy explained that Gunfire Weekends, as they were called
in the computer magazines, all appeared to be run with a
military flavour. 'Strict discipline. Order Groups at 09.00 hours,
Lights Out at 22.30, and all that. It was what happened after
Lights Out that became interesting.

'The oddballs are detailed to rooms near one another, and
always near Tigerbalm and Happy. The weekends cover three
nights. The oddballs all leave looking as though they've been
awake for a week. In fact they get very little sleep because around
midnight every night they're summoned to Old Bald Eagle's
private den, and there they stay, all night, working on their
own little games, two of which I'd like to get back into their
files before the dawn's early light.'

Bond told her to wait in his room while he went quietly down to the car, selected the equipment he needed and brought it back to the room. It took time, but the extra minutes spent reconnoitring the car park seemed well spent.

'Crikey!' Cindy looked at the Terror Twelve with undisguised pleasure. 'She certainly got it right. I only hope the circuit diagrams I provided were accurate.'

He'd buy that – Cindy monitoring the technology advances at Endor and providing Percy with all the information needed to build a computer identical to Holy's. Maybe he was but a part of this operation, only there to get the latest programs out. After that, others could step in and clean out the stables, armed with evidence provided by himself, Percy and Cindy.

With the keyboard, and hard laser drives plugged in, Bond took the first disk and booted up. The moment the first menu came on to the screen he knew what it was about: in a series of flashing green letters it read:

Phase One – Airport to Ken High Street
A. First girl driver
B. Second girl driver
C. Advance car
D. Trail car

He accessed the *First girl driver* and the screen showed him to be in heavy traffic, leaving Heathrow Airport and heading in to London. Ahead lay the small convoy of police and security vans. The program was obvious, and Bond flipped through the phases – *Turn Off; Kensington High Street: Phase One; Kensington High Street: Phase Two; Abort; Kensington High Street: Phase Violet Smoke*, and on to the getaway, passing options such as *Security Teams (Electrics)* and *Security Teams (Way Out)*. He did not need to run the whole simulation to know that the disk, currently resting in his top drive, was a training program for the Kruxator robbery.

Taking a virgin disk, Bond began to go through the careful

procedure of breaking down Jay Autem Holy's protection program in order to make a clean second copy of the original.

The process was very slow as Holy had used not only the regular, easy system of 'scribbling' on some sectors of the disk, but also the small routine Percy had shown Bond. In effect this was a program in itself, designed to crash the disk, making it completely useless, if anyone even attempted to copy it. Following Percy's tuition, Bond was able first to detect the routine and then remove it, line by line. Then he matched up his virgin disk in a format to copy exactly the original. The work took over an hour, but at the end he had a true clone of Holy's training program for the Kruxator robbery. He spent a further twenty minutes returning the protect program to the original disk.

The second of Cindy's disks was a similar training program, this time, they presumed, for the hijacking of an aircraft. As in fact there had been a monumental hijack of a specially chartered freight plane carrying newly printed money from the Royal Mint printers to several countries, the chances were that this was the blueprint for it.

Once more, the cloning process began, but this time with more urgency, for Cindy had become anxious about her return.

'There is one other thing,' she said, looking tired and concerned.

'Yes?' Bond grunted, not taking his eyes off the screen.

'Something very big's going on now. Not a robbery, I'm pretty sure of that, but a criminal, probably violent operation. There have been callers in the night, and I've heard several references to a special program.'

'What kind of special program?'

'I've heard the name only – they call it the Balloon Game, and there seem to be specialists involved.'

Bond was concentrating, writing back the protect program on to the hijack simulation original. 'They're all specialists, Cindy.'

'No, I've seen some of these guys. They're not all hoods and heavies. Some are like . . . are like pilots and parsons.'

'Parsons?'

'Well, not exactly. Doctors and dentists, if you like. Upright. Professional.'

'The Balloon Game?'

'I heard Tigerbalm use the expression, and one of the others – talking to Old Bald Eagle. Will you report it, please? I think it's something nasty.'

Bond said he would be getting the copies of these two pro-grams to London quickly. He'd mention the Balloon Game at the same time.

'You think they're using it now? Training on it?'

'Positive.'

'If we could get a copy . . .'

'Not a chance. Not yet, anyway.'

He fell silent, finishing off the job in hand. Presently he rattled off a description of Rolling Joe Zwingli. 'Ever see anyone like him around Endor?' he asked.

'General Zwingli. I recognise the description, and the answer's no. I had some garbled message from Percy that he's alive.' She paused, adding that this seemed incredible.

Bond completed his tasks and returned the original disks to Cindy and asked about the routine at the house. Did Jason and Dazzle ever go out? Or away? How many security people did they have around?

Yes, he went away for a couple of days about once a month. Always left and returned at night. Never left the house during the day, never showed his face in the village. Cindy invariably referred to Jay Autem as the Target, or Old Bald Eagle.

'Very cagey, our Target. Dazzle's out and about a great deal – in the village, over to Oxford, London, taking trips abroad. I suspect she's the liaison officer.'

'Where abroad?'

'Middle East, Europe. All over. Percy's got the list. I try to keep a track, mainly from hotel book matches or flight labels. But she's cagey as well. Gets rid of a lot of stuff before she comes home.'

As for the household, there was one Filipino boy and four security men. 'He has six genuine sales reps who wouldn't suspect a thing. But they're on the outside. The four security men double as reps and staff. It's very good cover. Would have had me fooled if I hadn't known better. They're all quiet, efficient guys – two cars between them, out and about a lot, managing the telephones, taking orders, distributing the genuine Gunfire Simulations packages. But two of them never leave the house. They work on the security in a strict rota. The electronics are highly sophisticated. Breakable, but clever. I mean, you have to know the system to fiddle it. What's more, as I've already told you, they alter the codings for every shift. You can only get in and out if you know the numbers for a particular six-hour period. Even then, the machines have to know your voice-print.'

'Visual?' Bond asked.

'Quite a lot – the main gates, large areas of the walls, front and rear of the house. You can only dodge the closed-circuit stuff at the back, and then only if you know the pattern. They change that with the lock codings, so you really do need to know your six-hour period to get in or out without being detected. An intruder wouldn't last three minutes.'

'Ever had any?'

'Intruders? Only a tramp, and one false alarm – at least they presume it was a false alarm.'

'Weapons?'

'I was around when the false alarm was triggered. Yes, one of the guys on duty had a hand gun. So I've seen one. There are probably more. James, can I get going? I can't afford to get caught with these disks on me. There are blanks in the cabinets . . .'

'On your way, Cindy, and good luck. I'll see you tonight. I'm coming for a little tournament with our Target. By the way, your friend Peter tipped me off about Jason's style of play . . .'

'He doesn't like to lose,' she said with a grin. 'Almost pathological, like a child. It's a matter of honour with him.'

Bond did not smile. 'And me,' he said softly. 'It's a matter of honour with me.'

It was past three-thirty in the morning. Bond packed up the equipment and took it down to the car, locking it away in the boot. Back in his room, he put the cloned programs in a FloppiPak disk mailer, smiling wryly at the frightful nomenclature of the trade. He addressed the label to himself at a Post Office box number, then weighed the small, flat package in his hand, making an intelligent guess as to weight. He stuck on what he estimated to be sufficient postage from a folder of stamps in his briefcase. He would have liked to deliver the package in person, but he was not going to leave anything to chance.

Sitting at the small dressing table, Bond next wrote a short note to Freddie on hotel paper.

Gone to Oxford for the morning. Didn't want to wake you, but will be back for lunch. How about a return match this afternoon?

J.

Stripping off, he ran a cold shower and stepped under it, holding his face against the stinging needle spray and gasping at the initial shock. After a minute or so, he added some warm water, soaped himself, then rubbed himself down, towelling his body briskly. Before shaving he climbed into his underwear, a pair of black Ted Lapidus cords and a black cotton rollneck. He strapped the ASP automatic, in its holster, so that it lay hard against his right hip. Last, he put on a light suede jacket and pushed his feet into the old favourite moccasins.

It was just getting light, the dark sky changing to grey and then that cold-washed pearl which heralds unsettled weather. With the detested FloppiPak in his briefcase, Bond went downstairs, left his key and the note for Freddie at the deserted reception and went out to the car.

The Bentley's engine growled into life at the first turn of the key, and he allowed it to settle to its normal, gentle purr, fastening the seatbelt and watching the red warning lights flick off one by one.

Releasing the foot brake, he slid the selector into Drive and let the car roll forward. If he took the Oxford road, turned on to the ring road, and then headed for the M40 he could be in London in ninety minutes.

It began to rain as he reached the big roundabout on the periphery of the ring road and took the dual carriageway, heading towards London. He was a mile or so along this stretch when the white Mercedes of the day before appeared in his mirror.

Bond cursed silently, tightened his seatbelt and moved his foot smoothly down on the accelerator. The car slid forward, gathering power, the speedometer rising to 100, then 120 miles per hour.

There was little traffic as he slid neatly in and out of the stray cars and lorries, mainly keeping to the fast lane.

The white Mercedes held back, but even at speed, Bond could not throw it off altogether. Ahead the signs came up for an exit. Flicking the indicator at the last moment, he left the dual carriageway still well in excess of the 100 miles per hour mark, the Bentley responding to his light control, holding the road during the turn. The Mercedes seemed to have disappeared. He hoped that the driver had not been able to reduce speed in time to get off the main highway.

Ahead the road narrowed, fir trees shadowing either side. A lumbering heavy transporter grumbled along at fifty behind a petrol tanker. The Bentley's speed dropped. As he rounded the next bend, Bond caught a flash of headlights, blinking on and off from a lay-by. The next time he looked there was another Mercedes hooking itself on to his tail.

They had radio contact, he thought, and probably five or six cars covering him. Taking the next left turn, he picked up the telephone and, without allowing his eyes to leave the road, punched out the numbers that would raise the Duty Officer at the Regent's Park Headquarters on a scrambled radio line.

The road narrowed. The second Mercedes was still there when he negotiated the next turn just as the Duty Officer answered.

'Gamesman flash for Dungeonmaster.' Bond spoke rapidly. 'Am being followed, south of Oxford. Important package for Dungeonmaster. Will attempt mail. Addressed myself. The Programmer is definitely involved all illegal actions as thought. Investigate Balloon Game. Speak to the Goddess.'

'Understood,' the Duty Officer said, and the line was closed.

As he took the next bend, Bond saw a village coming up and realised he had outdistanced the Mercedes. He pumped the footbrake, slowing the Bentley dramatically, looking ahead and to the left. The car was almost out of the village before he spotted the welcome brilliant red of a post box. The Bentley slid to a halt beside it, and Bond had his seatbelt off before the car had stopped rolling.

It took less than twenty seconds to slip the package into the box and return to the driving seat. He did not rebuckle the belt until the Bentley was already gathering speed and the Mercedes had appeared again in his driving mirror. He passed an electric milk float doing the early rounds, then he was once more in open country. As he reached a wooded stretch, Bond caught a glimpse of a picnic area sign, then saw two other cars emerge from the trees, their bonnets coming together to form a V, blocking his path.

'They're playing for keeps,' he muttered, ramming the footbrake, and hauling on the wheel with his left arm.

As the Bentley began to slew, broadside on, he was conscious of the white Mercedes close behind him.

The speedometer was touching sixty as the Bentley left the road, plunging in among the trees. Bond desperately guided the big car past the trunks, over bracken, zigzagging wildly and trying to negotiate a path that would bring him back to the road.

The first bullet made a grating, gouging sound on the roof,

and Bond could think only of the damage it would do to the coachwork. The second hit his rear offside tyre, sending over 5000lb of custom-built motor car side on into a tangle of bushes.

Slammed against the seatbelt, Bond reached simultaneously for the automatic pistol and the electric window button.

10

EREWHON

The ASP 9mm is a small, very lethal weapon. Essentially a scaled-down version of the Smith & Wesson Model 39, it has been in use with United States Intelligence Agencies for over a decade. With a recoil no greater than a Walther .22, it has the look of a target automatic rather than the deadly customised hand gun it really is. Armaments Systems and Procedures, the organisation which carried out the conversion, produced the weapon to exacting specifications: ease of concealment, a minimum eight-round capacity; reliability; an ammunition indicator using Lexon see-through butt grips, and an acceptance of all known 9mm ammunition.

The rounds in Bond's magazine were particularly unpleasant – Glaser Safety Slugs. A Glaser is a pre-fragmented bullet that contains several hundred No.12 shot suspended in liquid Teflon. The velocity of these slugs, fired from the ASP, is over 1700 feet per second. They will penetrate body armour before blowing, and a hit from a Glaser on any vital area of the body is usually fatal.

Bond fired two rounds from the lowered window almost before the car had come to a halt. He kept both eyes open, looking down the revolutionary back-mounted Guttersnipe sight, its triangular yellow walls giving instant target recognition.

Through the trees and bracken he could see several men leaving the cars. Others were trying to get the vehicles off the road.

Bond's rapid shots were aimed at the clear outline of a tall man in a dirty-white raincoat who was making for the Bentley. He did not stop to find out what happened to the target, but opened the door and rolled into the undergrowth.

Twigs and branches caught on his clothing and scratched his face, but Bond kept moving, determined to get as far away as possible from the Mulsanne Turbo. He rolled to the right, putting about twenty yards between himself and the car. Twisting round, flat on his belly, he brought the gun up and ready, his eyes constantly moving to cover a wide sweeping sight-line.

The other cars had been backed off the road and he guessed they now contained only their drivers. Two figures were visible, but almost by intuition he reckoned there had to be at least four others fanning out, moving low and trying to encircle him.

Bond lay quite still, allowing his breathing to settle. If his pursuers were methodical – and they probably were – they must eventually find him. It was even possible they could call up reinforcements. Certainly there had to be more men available. How could they have been certain of picking him up on the road, unless the Bentley had a location homer stuck on to it? Who were they? Some of Jay Autem Holy's men? There had to be a connection, yet Holy would have had a better opportunity to deal with him that evening, at Endor. Unless . . . unless Cindy had set him up, or been caught. If the latter, a watch had been put on him very quickly. At all events, Bond decided they would find him later rather than sooner. What he needed was time to make good his escape.

It had begun raining quite hard and you could hear the steady pattering from the branches. To attempt a move now would be suicidal. He was at least a hundred and fifty yards from the road, and even if he reached the other cars without being intercepted – which was unlikely – he would still be outnumbered three to one. He must wait, try to follow their search, and make sure nobody bounced him from behind.

He moved his head continually, looking from far left to far

right, then gently turning to watch the rear, all the time straining to catch any sound. The two men originally visible to his
front had disappeared, and the sounds of movement would now
be successfully blotted out by the rainfall.

Bond had been lying in cover for the best part of fifteen
minutes before he got a positive fix on any of his assailants. The
sharp crack of a dead branch and a flicker of movement on the
far left caught his ear and eye at the same moment. Slowly he
turned his head. There, not more than twenty paces away, a man
crouched against a tree, looking to the right of where Bond lay.
From the economical, alert manner, the way he kept low, using
the bottom of the tree trunk for cover, the small revolver held
steady in the right hand against left shoulder, the man looked
like a professional, a well-trained soldier. He was searching in
the calm, cautious manner of a hunter, examining every square
foot of ground within a specified arc. That meant there was
probably another like him to his left, or right, or both. What
was more, it could only be a matter of time before his eyes came
to rest on the ground where Bond lay.

The searcher wore olive green denim trousers and shirt, and a
military-style jacket. Moving each limb about half an inch at a
time, Bond began to turn. He wanted to get at least one shot in
before anyone closed on him.

There was another movement, this time to the right. Bond's
reflexes and intuition warned of danger, and he brought the ASP
up in the direction of this new threat.

The triple yellow walls, which angle to form the Guttersnipe
sight, fell automatically into their pattern, right on target, showing another figure running low between the trees, and much too
close for comfort. From the corner of his eye, he saw the first
man bringing his revolver up in a two-handed grip. Then he
heard the unmistakable click of a revolver hammer being drawn
back, very close behind him. The sharp burning cold of a muzzle
touched the side of his neck gently.

'Drop it, Mr Bond. Please don't try anything silly. Just drop the gun.'

Bond had no desire to get himself killed at this point in his career. He tossed the ASP on to the ground.

'Good.' The voice was soft, slightly lilting. 'Now, hands on the head, please.'

The two men who had been in Bond's sights were now standing, coming forward, the one to his left with arms outstretched, holding a snub-nosed revolver in the two-handed grip, the arms steady as iron bars. His eyes never left the captive. Bond was in no doubt that two bullets would reach him fast if he made any wrong move. The other came in quickly, scooping up the fallen ASP like a predatory bird swooping on to its prey.

'Right, now get to your feet very slowly,' the voice continued, the gun muzzle detaching itself from just behind Bond's ear. There was the sound of feet shuffling as the man stepped back. 'That manoeuvre was rather good, wasn't it? We knew roughly where you had gone to ground, so it was just a matter of showing you someone with stealth and another with speed. The lads went through that little farce three times before they found the right place. It's the kind of fieldcraft we teach. Please turn around.'

'Who teaches?' Bond demanded as he turned and faced a tall, well-built man in his mid-thirties with tight, curly hair, dark above matching jet eyes, a square face, a large nose and full lips. Women would find him attractive, Bond thought. The dark complexion was overlaid with a hard, sunbaked tan. It was the eyes that really gave him away. They had that particular look, as if, for years, they had searched horizons for the telltale sign of dust, or the sky for a speck, or an outcrop of rock for movement, or doorways and windows for muzzle flashes. Those eyes had probably been doing that kind of thing since childhood. Nationality? Who could tell? One of the Middle Eastern countries, but whether he came from Jerusalem, Beirut or Cairo was impossible to tell. Possibly a hybrid, Bond thought.

'Who teaches?' he asked again.

The young man lifted an eyebrow. 'You might get to find out, Mr Bond. Who knows?' The smile was not unfriendly. 'Now,' he said, 'we have to move you, and I cannot be certain you'll sit still.' He gave a short laugh. 'I rather think my superiors want you alive and in one piece, so would you take off your jacket and roll up your sleeve?'

Two more figures rose from the bushes as the senior man holstered his weapon, reaching into a hip pocket to bring out a hard oblong box.

One of the newcomers helped remove Bond's jacket while the other's hands rested firmly on his shoulders. Unresisting, Bond allowed them to roll up his sleeve while the leader filled a hypodermic syringe, lifting it so that the needle pointed upwards. A tiny squirt of colourless liquid arched into the air. Bond felt a damp swab on the upper part of his arm.

'It's okay,' the leader said with a smile. 'We do want you in one piece, I assure you. As the actress said to the bishop, just a little . . . er . . . a little jab.'

Somebody gave a loud laugh, and Bond heard another say something in a language he did not recognise. He did not even feel the needle slide home.

At first he thought he was in a helicopter, lying flat on his back with the machine bucking under him. He could hear the chug of the engine turning the rotor blades. Then, far away, came the rip of automatic firing. For a time, Bond drifted away again, then the helicopter sensation returned, accompanied by a series of loud explosions near at hand.

Opening his eyes, he saw an electric fan turning slowly above his head, and became aware of white walls and the simple metal bedframe on which he lay, fully dressed.

He propped himself on one arm. Physically he felt fine: no nausea, no headache, eyes focused properly. He held out his right hand, fingers splayed. There was no tremor. The room, bare of furniture apart from the bed, had just one door and a window covered with mesh inside and bars on the outside. Sunlight appeared dimly through the aperture.

As he swung his feet on to the floor he heard another distant explosion. He stood up and found his legs steady. Halfway to the door, there came the sound of more machine-gun fire – again at a distance. The door was locked, and he could make out little through the window. The mesh on the inside was a thick papery adhesive substance, which had been applied to the panes of glass, making it impossible to get any clear view. It would also prevent fragmentation from blast. Bond was convinced he was not in England. The temperature inside the little white room, even with the fan turning round and round, was not induced by the kind of heat you ever got in England, even in the most brilliant of summers. The sounds of small arms fire, punctuated by the occasional explosion, suggested he was in some war zone.

He tried the door again, then had a look at the lock. It was solid, well-made, and more than efficient. There would almost certainly be bolts on the outside too.

Methodically he went through his pockets but found nothing. They had cleaned him out. Even his watch was missing, and the metal bedframe appeared to be a one-piece affair. Given time, and some kind of lever, he might be able to force a piece of thick wire from the springs, but it would be an arduous business and he had no way of knowing how long he would be left alone.

When in doubt, do nothing, Bond thought.

He went back to the bed and stretched out, going over the events still fresh in his mind. The attempt to get away with the computer programs. Posting them. The trailing cars. The wood and his capture. The needle. He was the only one to have fired a shot. Almost certainly he had hit – probably killed – one of them. Yet, apart from their natural caution, they had been careful to make sure that he was unharmed. A connection between his visit to Jay Autem Holy and the current situation was probable, though not certain. Take nothing for granted. Wait for revelations. Expect the worst.

Bond lay there, mentally prepared, for the best part of twenty minutes. At last there came footsteps – muffled, as though boots crunched over earth, but the tread had a decidedly military sound. Bolts were drawn back and the door to Bond's room was unlocked and opened.

He caught a glimpse of sand, low white buildings and two armed men dressed in drab olive uniforms. A third person stepped into the room. He was the one who had administered the knock-out injection in the Oxfordshire wood. Now he wore uniform – a simple olive drab battledress, smart with no insignia or badges of rank. He had on desert boots and a revolver of high calibre holstered on the right of his webbing belt. A long sheathed knife hung from the belt on the left. His head was covered by a light brown, almost makeshift, *kaffiyeh* held in place by a red band. One of the men outside reached in and closed the door.

'Had a good sleep, Mr Bond?' The man's smile was almost infectious. As he looked up, Bond remembered his feelings about the eyes.

'I'd rather have been awake.'

'You're all right, though? No ill effects?'

Bond shook his head.

'Right. My name's Simon.' The man was crisp and business-like, extending a hand which Bond did not take. 'We hold no grudge over our man,' he said after a slight pause. 'You killed him, by the way. But he was being paid to risk his life.' He shrugged. 'We underestimated you, I fear. My fault. Nobody thought you'd be carrying a gun. After all, you're not in the trade any more. I guessed that, if you were armed, it would be for old time's sake, and nothing as lethal as that thing. It's unfamiliar to us, incidentally. What is it exactly?'

'My name is James Bond, formerly Commander, Royal Navy. Formerly Foreign Service. Now retired.'

Simon's face creased into a puzzled look for a moment.

'Oh, yes. I see. Name and rank.' He gave a one-note laugh. 'Sorry to disappoint you, Commander Bond, but you're not a prisoner of war. When you outran us in that beautiful motor car there was no way to let you know we came as emissaries. In friendship. A possible job.'

'You could have shouted. In the wood, you could have shouted, if that was the truth.'

'And would you have believed us?'

There was silence.

'Quite. No, I think not, Commander Bond. So we had to bring you in, alive and well, using only minimal force.'

Bond thought for a moment. 'I demand to know where I am and who you people are.'

'In good time. All in . . .'

'Where am I?' Bond snapped.

'Erewhon.' Simon gave a low chuckle. 'We go in for code names, cryptonyms. For safety, security, and our peace of mind – just in case you turn down the job, or even prove to be not quite the man we want. This place is called Erewhon. Now sir, the Officer Commanding would like a word.'

Bond slowly got off the bed, reached out and grasped Simon's left wrist, aware of the man's other hand moving swiftly to the revolver butt.

'Commander, I wouldn't advise . . .'

'Okay, I'm not going to attack you. I just don't recall having applied for a job. Not with anybody.'

'Oh, really? No, I suppose you haven't.' There was mocking ingenuousness in Simon's voice. 'But you're out of work, Commander Bond. That's true, surely?'

'Yes.'

'And, by nature, you're not an idle man. We wanted to – how would you say it? We wanted to put something your way.'

Bond eyed the man intently. 'Wouldn't it have been more

civilised to make your offer by invitation in England instead of this abduction?'

'The Officer Commanding Erewhon wishes to talk to you,' Simon said with a winning smile, as if that explained everything.

Bond appeared to think for a moment, then he nodded. 'I'll see your OC, then.'

'Good.'

Simon rapped on the door and one of the men outside opened up. As they stepped out, the two guards took station either side of Bond. He sniffed the air. It was warm, but clear. Rare. They must be fairly high above sea level. They were also in a small depression, the flat bed of a hollow, surrounded by hills. On one side the hills were low, a curving double mound, like a woman's breasts, but pitted with rock among the dry, sandy earth. The rest of the circle was more rugged, crests and peaks, running up several hundred feet, with outcrops of forbidding rock. The sun was high, almost directly above them. Along the flat sand bottom of the hollow was a series of low white buildings – one long rank with divisions, and another terrace with three shorter ranks at right angles, like a large letter E. Hard under the high ground there were other, similar buildings, though not so regimented. Simon led them across the five or six hundred yards towards one of these latter blocks.

Smoke drifted up from some of the smaller buildings. To Bond's left there was a firing range, with a group in uniform preparing to use it. Towards the round-topped hills, the sound of heavy explosions and small arms fire suddenly erupted from a clutter of gutted brick houses, which looked almost European. Figures dashed between these houses as though fighting a street battle.

As he turned at the noise, Bond also caught sight of some kind of bunker dug into the rock towards the top of one of the hills. A defensive position, he thought, almost impossible to attack from the air, though helicopter-borne landings presumably would be feasible.

'You like our Erewhon?' Simon asked cheerfully.

'Depends what you do here. You run package tours?'

'Almost.' Simon sounded quite amused.

They reached a building about the size of a modest bungalow. There was a notice, neatly executed, to the right of the entrance. OFFICER COMMANDING it said in several languages, including Hebrew and Arabic. The front door opened into a small, empty ante-room. Simon crossed to the one door at the far end, and knocked. A voice called out 'Come', and Simon gestured, smartly barking out,

'Commander James Bond, sir.'

With everything that had been going on, and with a myriad of questions unanswered, Bond would not have been shaken to find General Zwingli on the other side of the door, but the identity of the man seated behind the folding table which dominated the large office made him catch his breath with surprise. There was certainly some connection between this man and Zwingli, for the last time Bond had seen him was in the Salles Privées at Monte Carlo.

'Come in, Commander Bond. Come in. Welcome to Ere-whon,' said Tamil Rahani. 'Do sit down. Get the Commander a chair, Simon.'

I I

TERROR FOR HIRE

The room was functionally furnished: the folding table, four chairs and filing cabinet could have been found in the quarter-master's stores of any army in the world.

The furnishings also appeared to reflect the character of Tamil Rahani. From a distance, when Bond had seen him briefly in Monte Carlo, Rahani had looked like any other successful businessman – sleek, well-dressed, needle-sharp and confident. At close quarters, the confidence was certainly there, but that sleekness was clearly superficial. What stood out was a kind of dynamism – harnessed, and controlled. It was the air of self-discipline found in most good military leaders, a kind of quiet calm, and behind it an immense, unflinching resolve. Rahani certainly exhibited authority and a firm belief in his own ability.

As Simon brought the chair, and took one for himself, Bond quickly glanced around the office. The walls were lined with maps, charts, large posters displaying the silhouettes of aircraft, ships, tanks and other armoured vehicles. There were also year- and month-planners, their red, green and blue markers the only splashes of colour in the austere room.

'Don't I know you, sir?' Bond was careful to observe military courtesy. An aura of power and danger enveloped Rahani.

Rahani laughed, throwing his head back a little. 'You may have seen photographs of me in the newspapers,' Commander,' he said with a smile. 'We may speak about that later. At the moment I'd rather talk about you You have been highly recommended to us.'

'Really?'

Rahani tapped his teeth with a pencil. The teeth were perfect – white and regular, the moustache above them neatly trimmed.

'Let me be completely frank with you, Commander. Nobody knows whether you can be trusted or not. Everyone – and by that I mean most of the major intelligence communities of the world – knows that you have been an active officer of the British Secret Intelligence Service for a long time. You ceased to be either a member or active a short time ago. It is said that you resigned in a fit of bitterness.' He made a small questioning noise, like a hum, in the back of his throat. 'It is also said that *nobody* ever goes private from the SIS, the CIA, Mossad or the KGB. Is that the correct term? Going private?'

'So the spy writers tell us.' Bond maintained his attitude of indifference.

'Well,' Rahani continued, 'quite a few people wanted to find out the truth. A number of agencies would have liked to approach you. One very nearly did. But they got cold feet. They decided that you would probably rediscover your loyalty once put to the test, no matter how disaffected you felt.'

There was a pause, during which Bond remained poker-faced, until the Officer Commanding spoke again.

'You're either an exceptional actor, Commander, working under professional instructions, or you are genuine. What is undisputed is that you're a man of uncommon ability in your field. And you're out of work. If there is truth in the rumours surrounding your resignation, then it seems a pity to allow you to remain unemployed. The purpose of bringing you here is to test the story, and possibly to offer you a job. You would like to work? In intelligence, of course?'

'Depends.' Bond's voice was flat.

'On what?' Rahani said sharply, the man of authority showing through.

'On the job.' Bond's face relaxed a fraction. 'Look, sir. I don't wish to appear rude, but I was brought here against my will. Also, my previous career is nobody else's business but mine – and, I suppose, the people I used to work for. To be honest, I'm so fed up with the trade that I'm not at all sure I want to get mixed up in it again.'

'Not even as an adviser? Not even with a very high salary? With little to do, and less danger in doing it?'

'I just don't know.'

'Then would you consider a proposition?'

'I'm always open to propositions.'

Rahani took a long breath through his nose.

'An income in excess of a quarter of a million pounds sterling a year. The occasional trip at short notice to advise in another country. One week in every two months giving a series of lectures here.'

'Where's here?'

For the first time, Rahani's brow puckered with displeasure. 'In good time, Commander. As I've said, in good time.'

'Advise on what? Lecture on what?'

'Lecture on the structure and methods of the British Secret Intelligence Service, and the Security Service. Advise on the intelligence, and security aspects of certain operations.'

'Operations carried out by whom?'

Rahani spread his hands. 'That would depend. It would also alter from operation to operation. You see, the organisation I command bears no allegiance to any one country, group of people or ideal. We are – a much-used word, but the only one – we are apolitical.'

Bond waited, as though not yet prepared to commit himself.

Rahani finally gave in. 'I am a soldier. I have been a mercenary in my time. I am also a highly successful businessman. We have certain things in common, I think, one of them being a liking for money. Some time ago, in co-operation with one or two like-minded people, I saw the possibility of earning some very profitable returns by going into the mercenary business. Being apolitical myself, owing nothing to ideologies or beliefs, it was easy. Plenty of countries and revolutionary groups need specialists. A particular man or a group of men – even a planning group, and the soldiery to carry out the plan.'

'Rent-a-Terrorist,' Bond said, with a touch of distaste. 'Who does not dare, hires someone else to dare for them. A truly mercenary activity, in every sense.'

'Well put. But you'd be surprised, Commander Bond. The terrorist organisations are not our only customers. Bona fide governments have approached us too. Anyway, as a former intelligence officer you cannot allow yourself the luxury of politics or ideals.'

'I can allow myself the luxury of opposing certain ideals. Of disagreeing, and intensely disliking them,' Bond put in.

'And, if our information is to be believed, you have an intense dislike for the British and American method of intelligence – yes?'

'Let's just say I'm disappointed that an official organisation can call me to question after so many years of loyal service.'

'Don't you ever feel that revenge could be sweet?'

'I'd be a liar if I said it hadn't crossed my mind, but it's never been an obsession. I don't harbour grudges.'

'We shall need your co-operation, and your decision. You understand what I mean?' Rahani made the querying, humming noise again.

Bond nodded, and said he was no fool: having disclosed the existence and purpose of his organisation, Tamil Rahani was committed to making a decision about Bond. If he offered a job, and if Bond accepted, there would be no problem. If, however, he decided Bond was a risk, or his motives were in doubt, there could be only one answer.

Rahani heard him out.

'You won't mind if I ask a few pertinent questions, then?'

'What do you call pertinent?'

'I'd like to know the things you would not discuss with the Press. The *real* reason for your resignation, Commander Bond. An inter-department disagreement, I believe you said. Accusations, which were withdrawn, but taken most seriously by yourself.'

'If I don't choose to tell you?'

'Then we have to conclude that you are not trustworthy, my friend. A conclusion which may have unpleasant consequences.' Rahani smiled.

Bond went through the process of looking as though he was giving the situation some thought. With M and Bill Tanner he had put together a story that would hold water up to a point. To prove or disprove it would mean getting classified information from the Judicial Branch, which comprised a number of experienced barristers retained by the Service; also from three individuals working in the Registry, and from someone who had easy access to the documents held by S Department. After a few moments' silence Bond gave a short nod. 'Right. If you want the truth . . .'

'Good. Tell us then, Commander Bond.' Rahani's voice and manner were equally bland.

He told the story, just as they had concocted it in M's office. Over a period of some six months it had been discovered that several highly sensitive files had been taken from the Service HQ and kept out overnight. It was an old story, and one that was technically plausible, even allowing for the stringent security spot checks, and signing in and out of files. However, the system was double-checked by an electronic bar code, appended to each file, which was scanned every time the file was taken out or returned. The files went through a machine that read the code and stored the information in the Registry databank, which was examined at the end of each month. It was impossible to alter the bar codes on the files or to duplicate them. But because the information stored away on the big computer tapes was read out only at the end of each month, anyone could return a dummy file each night, putting back the original the following night. By alternating dummy and original you could examine around twenty files in a month before the tampering would be discovered. This, Bond maintained, was what had happened, though Registry had spent so much time cross-checking and looking at the data because they imagined it to be a program error in the computer, that a further week had passed before a report went up to Head of Service.

In all, only eight files had been at risk. But, on the relevant dates, James Bond had been one of those with access to the files. Five people were under suspicion, and they had hauled Bond in before anybody else.

'Someone of my rank and experience would normally be given the courtesy of a private interview with the Head of Service,' he said, his tone verging on anger. 'But no. It didn't seem to matter that the other four were junior, relatively inexperienced and without field records. It was as if I was singled out because of my position, because I had been in the field, because of my experience.'

'You were actually accused?' It was Simon who asked.

Bond allowed the anger to boil up and break the surface. 'Oh, yes. Yes, I was accused. Before they even talked to anyone else they carted in a couple of very good interrogators, and a QC. *You removed these files from the headquarters building, Commander Bond. Why? Did you copy them? Who asked you to take them?* It went on for two days.'

'And did you take them from the building, Commander?'

'No, I did not,' Bond almost shouted. 'And it took them another two days to haul in the other four, and then a day for Head of Registry to come back off leave and remember that special permission had been given to one officer to take the wretched files over for study by a Civil Service mandarin – adviser to the Ministry. They had left spaces in the records, just to keep the data neat. Head of Registry was supposed to put a special code into the databank. But he was off on leave, and forgot about it. Nobody had a go at him, or offered his head on a salver.'

'So no files went missing at all. You got an apology, of course?'

'Not immediately.' Bond glowered, like a schoolboy. 'And nobody seemed at all concerned about my feelings. Head of Service didn't appear even to understand why I got annoyed.'

'So you resigned? Just like that?'

'More or less.'

'It's a very good story.' Tamil Rahani looked pleased. 'But it will be difficult to prove, if I know anything about government departments.'

'Exceptionally difficult,' Bond agreed.

'Tell me, what did the files in question contain?'

'Ah.' Bond tried to look as charming as possible. 'Now you're really asking me to betray.'

'Yes.' Rahani was quite matter-of-fact.

'Mainly updated material on the disposition of Eastern Bloc tactical forces. One concerned agents on the ground and their proximity to the Eastern bases.'

Rahani's eyebrows twitched. 'Sensitive. I see. Well, Commander, I shall make a few enquiries. In the meantime, perhaps Simon will show you around Erewhon, and we'll continue to have little talks.'

'You mean interrogations?'

Rahani shrugged. 'If you like. Your future career depends on what you tell us now. Quite painless, I assure you.'

As they reached the door, Bond turned back. 'May I ask *you* a question, sir?'

'Of course.'

'You bear a striking resemblance to a Mr Tamil Rahani, chairman of Rahani Electronics. I believe you've been in Monte Carlo recently?'

Rahani's laugh had all the genuine warmth of an angry cobra. 'You should know, Commander. You were raising a fair amount of hell at the gaming tables on the Côte d'Azur at the time, I think.'

'Touché, sir.'

Bond followed Simon out into the sunshine. They went first to a mess hall where about eighty people were enjoying a lunch of chicken cooked with peppers, onions, almonds and garlic. Everyone wore the same olive uniform. Some carried side arms. There were men and women, mainly young, and from many different countries. They sat in pairs or teams of four. That was how the training went, Simon explained. They worked with a partner or in teams. Sometimes two teams would be put together, if the work demanded it. Some of the pairs were training to be loners.

'Doing what?' Bond asked.

'Oh, we cover the usual spectrum. Big bang merchants, take away artists, removal men, monopoly teams. You name it, we do it – electricians, mechanics, drivers, all the necessary humdrum jobs too.'

Bond identified a number of different tongues being spoken in the hall – German, French, Italian. There were also Israelis, Irish, and even English he was told. He almost immediately identified a pair of German terrorists whose names and details were on file with his Service, MI5 and at Scotland Yard.

'If you want anonymity, I shouldn't use those two in Europe,' he told Simon quietly. 'They've both got star billing with our people.'

'That's good. Thank you. We prefer unknowns, and I had a feeling about that couple. Everyone has had some field work behind them when they come here, but we don't like faces.' Simon gave a knowing grin. 'We do need them though. Some have to be lost, you know. It comes in handy during training.'

Throughout the afternoon, they walked around the well-equipped training area, and Bond experienced the odd sensation of having seen all this before. It took an hour or so to work out exactly what was wrong. These men and women were being trained in techniques he had seen used by the SAS, Germany's GSG9, the French GIGN, and several other élite units dealing with anti-terrorist activities. There was one difference, however. The trainees at Erewhon were receiving expert tuition on how to counter anti-terrorist action.

Apart from classes in weaponry of all kinds, special attention was paid to hijacking and takeover. They even had two flight simulators in the compound. One building was devoted solely to the techniques of bargaining with authorities while holding either hostages or kidnap victims. The skills were being taught extremely thoroughly.

One of the most spectacular training aids lay around the gutted buildings Bond had noticed earlier. Here a team of four would be taught how to fight off attempted rescues employing all the known counter-terrorist techniques. It was disturbing to note that most eventualities appeared to be covered.

That night Bond slept again in the same sparsely furnished room where he had first woken. On the following day, the interrogation began. It was conducted on a classic one-to-one basis – Tamil Rahani and James Bond – with Rahani asking seemingly ordinary questions that were, in fact, attempts to ferret out highly sensitive information about Bond's Service.

Rahani began with reasonably harmless stuff, such as organisation and channels of command. Soon, detail was being called for, and Bond had to use all his native ingenuity to give the appearance of telling everything, at the same time keeping back really vital information.

Rahani was like a terrier. Just when Bond thought he had managed to avoid giving some piece of information, Rahani would change tack, going in a circle to return to the nub of the question. It became all too obvious that once they had milked him dry, Bond would be quietly thrown to the wolves.

On the sixth day Rahani was still hammering away at the same questions concerning details of protection for heads of state, the Prime Minister, the Queen and other members of the Royal

Family. This was not part of Bond's own work, or the work of his Service, but Rahani quite rightly assumed that Bond would know a great deal about it. He even wanted names, possible weaknesses in those assigned to such duties, and the kind of schedules they worked. At about five o'clock in the afternoon, a message was brought in. Rahani read it, then slowly folded the paper and looked at Bond.

'Well, Commander, it seems your days here are numbered. There is a job for you back in England. Something very important is at last coming to fruition, and you are to be part of it. You are on salary as from now.'

He picked up one of his telephones and asked for Simon to come over as quickly as possible. Bond had learnt by now that they used first names at Erewhon for everyone except the Officer Commanding.

'Commander Bond is with us,' he told Simon. 'There's work for him, and he leaves for England tomorrow. You will escort him.' An odd look passed between the two men before Rahani continued. 'But, Simon, we have yet to see the gallant Commander in action. Would it be a good idea to put him through the Charnel House?'

'He'd like that, I'm sure, sir.'

The Charnel House was a gallows-humour nickname for the gutted buildings they used for training against counter-terrorist forces. Simon said he would set things up, and they walked the short distance to the area, where Simon left to make the arrangements. Ten minutes later, he returned, taking Bond inside the house.

Though the place was gutted and bore the marks of many simulated battles, it had been remarkably well built. There was a large entrance hall inside the solid main door. Two short passages to left and right led to large rooms, which were uncarpeted, but contained one or two pieces of furniture. At the top of a solid staircase was a wide landing with one door. Through this a long passage ran the length of the house with doors on the facing wall leading into two rooms built directly above those on the ground floor. Simon led Bond upstairs. 'There will be a team of four. Blank ammunition, of course, but real flash-bangs.' Flash-bangs were stun grenades, not the most pleasant thing to be near on detonation. 'The brief is that they know you are somewhere upstairs.' Simon pulled out the ASP 9mm. 'Nice weapon, James. Very nice. Who would think it has the power of a .44 Magnum?'

'You've been playing with my toys.'

'Couldn't resist it. There – one magazine of blanks, and one spare. Use your initiative, James. Good luck.' He looked at his watch. 'You have three minutes.'

Bond quickly reconnoitred the building and placed himself in the upper corridor, since it had no windows. He stayed close to the door which opened on to the landing, but was well shielded by the corridor wall. He was crouched against the wall when the stun grenades exploded in the hallway below – two ear-splitting crumps, followed by several bursts of automatic fire. Bullets hacked and chipped into the plaster and brickwork on the other side of the wall, while another burst almost took the door beside him off its hinges.

They were not using blanks. This was for real, and he knew with sudden shock, that it was as he had earlier deduced. He was being thrown to the wolves.

12

RETURN TO SENDER

Two more explosions came from below, followed by another heavy burst of fire. The second team of two men was clearing the ground floor. Bond could hear the feet of the first team on the stairs. In a few seconds there would be the dance of death on the landing – a couple of stun grenades or smoke canisters would be thrown through the door to his right, then lead would hose down the passage, taking him on that short trip into eternity.

Simon's voice kept running in his head like a looped tape: 'Use your initiative . . . Use your initiative . . .' Was that a hint? A clue? There was certainly something of a nudge in the tone he had adopted.

Move. Bond was off down the corridor, making for the room to his left. He had some vague idea that he might leap from the window. Anything to remove himself from the vicious hailstorm of bullets.

He took rapid strides into the room and, trying to make as little noise as possible, closed the door, automatically sliding a small bolt above the handle. He started to cross the floor, heading for the windows, clutching the useless ASP as though his life depended on it. As he sidestepped a chair, he saw them – two ASP magazines, cutaway matt black oblongs, lying on a rickety table between the high windows. Grabbing at the first, he saw immediately that they were his own reserves, both full, loaded with Glasers.

There is a fast routine for reloading the ASP, a fluent movement that quickly jettisons an empty magazine, replacing it with a full one. Bond went through the reload procedure in a matter of five seconds, including dropping his eyes to check that a live round had entered the chamber.

He performed the reloading on the move, finally positioning himself hard against the wall to the left of the door. The team would leap in after the grenades had accomplished their disorientating effect, one to the left and one right. They would be firing as they came, but Bond gambled on their first bursts going wide across the room.

Flattening himself against the wall, he held the powerful little weapon at arm's length in the two-handed grip, at the same time clutching the spare magazine almost as an extension to the butt.

They were making straight for this room. As he reloaded, Bond had been conscious of the bangs and rattle of their textbook assault through the landing door. Bullets spat and splintered the woodwork to his right. A boot smashed in the handle and broke the flimsy bolt, while a pair of stun grenades hit the bare boards, making a heavy clunk, one of them rolling for a split second before detonation.

He closed his eyes, head turning slightly to avoid the worst effect – the flash that temporarily blinds – though nothing could stop the noise which seemed to explode from within his own cranium, putting his head in a vice, and ringing in his ears like a magnified bell. It blotted out all external sounds, even that of his own pistol as he fired, and the death-rattle of the submachine guns as the two-man team stepped through the lingering smoke.

Bond acted purely by intuition. At the first movement through the door he sighted the three little yellow triangles on the dark moving shape. He squeezed the trigger twice, resighted and squeezed again. In all the four bullets were off in less than three seconds – though the whole business appeared to be frozen in time, slowed down like a cinematic trick so that everything happened with a ponderous, even clumsy, brutality.

The man nearest Bond came through, leaping to his left, the wicked little automatic weapon tucked between upper arm and ribcage, the muzzle already spitting fire as he identified and turned towards his target. Bond's first bullet caught him in the neck, tearing through flesh, bone, arteries and sinews, hurling the man sideways, pushing him, the head lolling, as though it was being torn away from its body. The second slug entered the head, which exploded, leaving a cloud of fine pink and grey matter hanging in the air. The third and fourth bullets both caught the second man in the chest, a couple of inches below the windpipe. He was swinging outwards, and to his right, realising too late where the target was situated, the gun in his hand spraying bullets towards the window.

The impact lifted the man from his feet, knocking him back so that, for a split second he was poised in mid-air, angled at forty-five degrees to the floor, the machine-pistol still firing and ripping into the ceiling as a mushroom of blood and flesh spouted from the torn chest.

Because of his temporary deafness, Bond felt as though he stood outside the action, as if watching a silent film. But his experience pushed him on: two down, he thought, two to go. The second team almost certainly would be covering the entrance hall, and may even be coming to the assistance of their comrades at this moment.

Bond stepped over the headless corpse of the first intruder, his foot almost slipping in the lake of blood. It always amazed Bond how there was so much blood in one man. This was something they did not show in movies, or even news film – over a gallon of blood which fountained from a human body when violently cut to pieces.

In the doorway, he paused for a second, ears straining to no effect, for his head still buzzed as though a hundred electric doorbells were ringing inside his skull.

Glancing down, he saw that the second man still had a pair of grenades tucked firmly into his belt, hooked on by the safety levers. He slid one out, removed the pin, and holding it in his left hand advanced down the corridor towards the landing door, calculating the amount of force he would need to hurl the grenade down the stairs. It had to be right, for he would not get a second chance.

He paused, just short of the landing door. Something made him turn – that sixth sense which, over the years, was now fine-tuned to most emergencies. He spun round just in time to see a figure emerging gingerly from the room, negotiating his way through the gore and shattered bodies on the far side of the door. Later, Bond reasoned they had planned some kind of pincer manoeuvre when they heard additional shots, one man scaling the wall to attack through the window, the other mounting the stairs.

Bond let off two shots at the man in the doorway, both aimed at the centre of the target, while with his left hand he lobbed the stun grenade out of the landing door in the direction of the staircase. He saw the man in the doorway spin as though caught by a whirlwind. In the same instant, he was aware of the flash from the landing.

There were only two rounds left in the first magazine. In five seconds Bond replaced it with the fully charged one. Then he took two paces through the door, firing as he went, two slugs going nowhere while he located his target.

The last man was struggling at the bottom of the stairs, for the grenade had caught him napping. From the scorch marks and his agonised beating at the smouldering cloth around his loins, it was obvious that the grenade had hit him in the groin while he was on the stairs.

Still deafened, Bond saw the man's mouth opening and closing, his face distorted. From the top of the stairs Bond shot him once, neatly blowing off the top of his head so that he fell on to his back, moving a foot or so on impact, with his brains spilling out over the dirty entrance hall floor.

Quietly, Bond retraced his footsteps, once more stepping over the now-larger sprawl of bodies, and crossing to the window. Below, about twenty yards away, Tamil Rahani stood with Simon and half a dozen members of Erewhon's permanent staff. They were quite still, heads held as though listening. There was no sign of an unholstered weapon, and Bond could not see a gun trained on the house from any vantage points.

He moved back from the window, not wanting to show himself, yet uncertain of the safest way to get out of the place. He had gone only two steps, when the decision was partially made for him.

'Are you still with us, Commander Bond?' Rahani's voice drifted up from outside, followed by Simon calling, 'James? Did you figure it out?'

He returned to the window, standing to one side, showing as little of his head as possible. They were all in the same place. Still there were no weapons visible.

Withdrawing, Bond shouted, 'You tried to kill me, you bastards. Let's make it fair. I'll take you on – one at a time.'

He dropped to the ground and snake-crawled below the window, along the wall to the next aperture. They were all looking at the first window as he fired, putting the bullet about ten yards in front of them, kicking up a great cloud of dust.

'Right, Bond.' It was Tamil Rahani calling. 'Nobody wanted to do you any harm. It was a test, that's all. A test of your efficiency. Just come out now. The test is over.'

'I want one of you, unarmed. Just one – Simon, if you like. In now. At the front. Otherwise I start taking you out, very quickly.' Bond took a quick peep through the window. Simon was already unbuckling his belt, letting it fall to the ground as he walked forward.

Seconds later, Bond was at the top of the stairs, and Simon

stood in the entrance hall, hands on his head, looking up at Bond with some admiration.

'What's going on exactly?' Bond asked.

'Nothing. You did as we expected. Everyone told us how good you were, so we sent in four expendable men. Two of them were the ones you pointed out to me the other day, the Germans you said were known faces. We have others like them. This is a standard exercise.'

'Standard? Telling the victim only blank ammunition is being used?'

'Well, you soon discovered you had live rounds, like the others. They also thought they had blanks.'

'But I had live ammunition only if I could find it, which I did partially by luck.'

'Rubbish, James. You had the real thing from the word go, and there were spare magazines all over the place. Can I come up?'

Keeping his hands on his head, Simon slowly mounted the stairs, while Bond began to wonder. Fool, he said to himself. You took the man's word for it. He said you had blanks, but . . .

Five minutes later, Simon had proved his point, first by retrieving Bond's original magazine, which was fully loaded with Glasers, and then by showing him other full magazines on the corridor floor and in the second room upstairs, as well as on the landing. Even with live ammunition, it had been an exceptionally dangerous business. One man against four armed with, as it turned out, MP 5K submachine guns.

'I could have been wiped out within seconds.'

'But you weren't, were you, James? Our information was that you would get out of this kind of challenge alive. It just shows that our informants were correct.'

They walked down the stairs and out into the warm air, which felt very good. Bond had a feeling that he was, indeed, lucky to be alive. He also wondered if his luck was merely a stay of execution.

*

'And if I had died in there?'

Rahani did not smile at the question. 'Then, Commander Bond, we would have had only one body to bury instead of four. You lived; you showed us your reputation is well-deserved. Here life and death is of equal importance, in that it is only survival that matters.'

'And it was, as Simon said, a challenge? A test?'

'More of a test.'

They had dined alone, the three of them. Now they sat in Tamil Rahani's office.

'Please believe me.' The Officer Commanding Erewhon made an open gesture with his hands. 'I would not have put you through this ordeal had it been up to me.'

'It's your organisation. You were offering me a job.'

Rahani did not look him in the eye.

'Well,' he said, his voice low, 'I have to be perfectly frank with you. Yes, the founding of an organisation which rents out mercenary terrorists *was* originally my idea. Unhappily, as so often happens in cases like this, I needed specialist assistance. That meant taking in partners. The result is I get a large return, but . . . well, I take my orders from others.'

'And in this case your orders were?'

'To see if you were trustworthy and could be used, or merely an undercover plant. To obtain information from you that we could easily test, and then – if that was okayed – to put you up against a real challenge, to see if you could survive a potentially lethal situation.'

'And I've passed on all points?'

'Yes. We are well satisfied. Now, you can be returned to our planners. It was true when I said there was a job waiting for you. There has been from the word go. That is why you were brought here, where we have facilities. You see, once here, if you had turned out to be . . . what do you people say? A double? Is that right?'

Bond nodded.

'If you had been exposed as a double, we had the facilities here for losing you. Permanently.'

'So, what's this job you have for me?'

'It is a large and complex operation. But one thing I can tell you.' Rahani looked up at Bond, his eyes blank as though made of glass. 'What is being planned at the moment will be the terrorist coup of the decade, even the century. If things proceed normally, it will spark off the ultimate revolution. A unique and complete change in the course of world events. The beginning of a new age. And those of us taking part in it will have a privileged position in the society that will emerge.'

'I saw the film.'

Simon rose and went over to the filing cabinet, where there were a few bottles. He poured himself a generous glass of wine, then disappeared from view.

'Scoff, Commander Bond. But I think even you will find this to be an operation without parallel in history.'

'And it won't work without me?' Bond raised an eyebrow sardonically.

'I did not say that. But it may not work without somebody like you.'

'Okay.' He leaned back in his chair. 'So tell me all about it.'

'I'm afraid I can't do that.' Rahani's cold eyes bored into him, so that, for a second or two, Bond thought the man was trying out some elementary hypnosis.

'So?'

'So, you have to be returned. You have to go back.'

'Back? Back to where?'

Too late Bond felt Simon's presence behind him.

'Back where you came from, James.'

Bond was conscious of the small, sharp pinch through his shirt, on his arm just below the right shoulder.

Tamil Rahani continued to speak.

'We're not talking about stories dreamed up by pulp novelists. No blackmail through concealed nuclear devices hidden in the heart of great Western cities; no plots to kidnap the President, or hold the world to ransom by setting all the major currencies at naught. We're not talking about extortion; neither . . . are . . . we . . .' His voice slowly receded, blurred, and then stopped.

13

THE NUMBERS RACKET

The sky was grey, almost leaden. He could see it through the window – the sky and part of an old apple tree. That was all.

Bond had woken from what seemed to be natural sleep. He was still fully dressed, and the ASP, complete with holster and one extra clip of ammunition, lay on the bedside table. The room appeared to be a genuine English bedroom – white gloss paint on the woodwork and Laura Ashley wallpaper, with a contrasting fabric for curtains; only most of the window was bricked up, and the door would not budge when he tried to open it.

There was a depressing sense of *déjà vu*. He had been along this road before, only last time it was Erewhon. Rahani had said they had accepted him, but he wondered how and why. Certainly the long interrogation sessions had been searching – M had instructed him to give away anything they could check on, even if it was highly sensitive. Fences, his Chief maintained, could be mended later. But what would be the state of play by the time they came to mend fences? At Erewhon preparations were going forward for something earth-shattering. What was it that Rahani had said – 'A unique and complete change in the course of world events'? The dream of revolutionaries: to change history, to crush the status quo, to alter it in order to build a new society. Well, Bond thought, it had been done before, but only within countries: Russia was the prime example, though Hitler's rise in Germany had been a revolution as well. The problem with revolutions was that the ideal usually fell short because of human frailty. M often expounded such theories.

Rahani had told him that he, Bond, or somebody like him, would be essential to whatever was about to take place. They needed someone with the skills, the contacts and the knowledge of an experienced Secret Intelligence field officer. What part of those skills, or what special knowledge was required?

He was still pondering on these things when somebody knocked at the door and a key turned in the lock.

Cindy Chalmer looked bright and crisp. She wore a laboratory coat over jeans and shirt, and was carrying a large tray.

'Breakfast, Mr Bond,' she said, beaming at him.

In the background, he could see a tall, muscular man.

Bond nodded towards him. 'Someone to watch over me?'

'And me, I guess.' She set the tray down on the end of the bed. 'Can't be too careful with hot shots like you around. Nobody knew what you'd like, so Dazzle did the full English breakfast – bacon, eggs, sausages, toast, coffee.' She lifted the silver cover from the steaming plate, holding the inside towards Bond. There was a folded paper neatly taped to the inside.

'That'll do fine.' He gave her a nod. 'Do I call room service when I've finished?'

'Don't call us, we'll call you,' she said brightly. 'We shall, Mr Bond. I gather the Professor wants to talk to you later. Good to see you feeling better. They said you had a nasty bump when you went off the road. The Professor was genuinely worried, that's why he persuaded the hospital to let him bring you here.'

'Very good of him.'

She lingered by the door. 'Well, it's nice to know we'll all be working together.'

'Good to have a job in these difficult times,' Bond countered, not knowing how much Cindy knew or believed. Had they told her he'd been in a motor accident? That he was being given a job at Endor? Well, presumably the latter was more or less true.

Bond waited until the key had been pushed home in the lock.

There was no other sound, no retreating footsteps, for the passage outside, like this room, was overlaid with thick carpet.

The paper came away easily from the inside of the lid. Cindy had filled it with small, neat writing and, in spite of the steam, the ink had not run. The note started abruptly, without any salutation.

I don't know what's happened. They say you've had a car smash, but I don't know whether to believe them. They brought your Bentley back here, and there's been a lot of talk about you joining the team as a programmer. I wondered if they knew you had computer equipment with you, and felt you would not want them to find it. Very difficult, but I got hold of the Bentley's keys and cleaned out the boot. All your private stuff is now hidden in the garage and not likely to be found, unless we're unlucky. A good thing I did it straight away, because security's been tightened for the weekend. A lot of people are coming down, and from what I've heard, the game I told you about (remember the balloons?) is going to be in use. It is possible that I may be able to get hold of it. Do you wish to copy? Or is that superfluous now that you are One of Us?

C.

So, the place was going to be crowded, the Balloon Game to be used. Bond was essential. Therefore, if the Balloon Game was a training simulation for the operation, then Bond and the Game were closely connected. QED.

He tore the message into tiny pieces, and ate them with the bacon and some toast. He could not stomach the eggs or sausage, but the coffee was good, and he drank four cupfuls, strong and black.

There was a small bathroom attached to his bedroom. Set neatly on the glass shelf above the handbasin were his razor and his favourite cologne. Already he had seen his weekend case beside the small wardrobe. On examination he discovered his clothes had all been washed and neatly pressed.

Don't believe it all, he told himself. On the face of it, he was trusted; his weapon, shaving kit and clothes were intact. But they kept the door locked and there was no easy way out of the window. It was possible that they only wanted him to believe he had been accepted.

He showered, shaved and changed, putting on fresh casual clothes that allowed him to move easily and fast. Even the ASP was strapped to his right hip by the time a second knock and the turning of the key announced the arrival of two muscular men whose faces were familiar from Cindy's description – Tigerbalm Balmer and Happy Hopcraft.

'Mornin', Mr Bond.' Tigerbalm greeted him with a smile, his eyes not meeting Bond's but sliding around the room, as though measuring it up for a robbery.

'Hallo, James, nice ter meecher.' Happy stuck out a hand, but Bond pretended not to notice.

'Balmer and Hopcraft,' Tigerbalm said. 'At your service. The Professor wants a word.'

Behind the expensive mohair suits and the cheerful bonhomie lay a hint of menace. Just by looking at them, you could see that this pair would have your head stuffed and mounted if it suited them, or they had instructions from anyone paying them enough.

'Well, if the Professor calls, we must answer.' Bond looked at the key clutched in Tigerbalm's hand. 'That really necessary?'

'Orders,' Happy said.

'Let's go and see the Professor then.'

They did not exactly crowd him as they went downstairs to the working area. There was no pushing or frogmarching, but their presence had a certain intimidating effect. Bond felt that one false move – any inclination to go in another direction – would bring about a fast, restraining action. There was no sign of Cindy or Peter. But St John-Finnes sat at his desk, the large computer keyboard in front of him and the VDU giving out a glow of colour.

'James, it's nice to have you back.' He signalled with his head that Tigerbalm and Happy should leave, then gestured to an easy chair.

'Well,' he went on brightly when they were settled. 'I'm sorry you were put to some inconvenience.'

'I could have been killed quite easily.' Bond spoke in a level, calm manner.

'Yes. Yes, I'm sorry about that. But in the event it was you who did the killing, I gather.'

'Only because I had to. Habits take a long time to die. I think my reactions are reasonably fast.'

The narrow, birdlike head moved up and down in comprehension. 'Yes, the reports all say you're rather good. You must understand that we had to be sure of you. I mean, one error and a great deal of money, and planning, would have been in jeopardy.'

Bond said nothing.

'Anyway, you passed with flying colours. I'm glad, because we need you. You're now aware of the connection between things here at Endor, and the training camp, Erewhon?'

'I understand you and your partner, Mr Tamil Rahani, run a rather strange enterprise, hiring mercenaries to terrorist and revolutionary groups,' Bond stated flatly.

'Oh, a little more than that.' His manner was now benign, smiling and nodding. 'We can offer complete packages. A group comes to us with an idea and we do everything else, from raising the money to performing the operation. For instance, the job you have been recruited for has been on the drawing board some time now, and we stand to gain a great deal from it.'

Bond said he realised that he had been vetted, and he knew there was a job for him within the organisation, and connected to an operation, 'But I've no idea of the . . .'

'Details? No, of course you haven't. Just as in your old Service people work on a need-to-know basis, so we must be exceptionally careful, particularly with this current work. No one person is in possession of the full picture, with the exception of Colonel

Rahani and myself, of course.' He made a slight movement of the fingers and head, which was meant to convey modesty. It was a curiously oriental gesture, as though he wished Bond to realise that he was really unworthy to be granted the honour of knowing such plans. Bond also noted that it was now *Colonel* Rahani, and he wondered where that title came from.

'. . . especially careful concerning you, I fear,' St John-Finnes was saying. 'Our principals were very much against giving you a situation of trust, but – since Erewhon – we have made them think twice.'

'This job? The one you've recruited me for . . .' Bond started.

'Has been in the making for a considerable time. A large amount of money was needed, and our principals were, shall we say, short of funds. This suited us. We're packagers, Bond. So we packaged some moneymaking projects to finance the main thrust.'

'Hence the Kruxator Collection and other high-tech robberies.'

Jay Autem Holy, alias St John-Finnes, remained icy cold. Only in his eyes could Bond detect a tiny wariness. 'You come to interesting deductions, my dear Bond. For one who knows nothing . . .'

'Stab in the dark.' Bond's face betrayed nothing. 'After all, there have been several imaginative robberies lately – all with the same handwriting. A case of putting two and two together, and maybe coming in with the correct answer.'

Holy made a noncommittal grunt. 'I'll accept that you're clean, Bond. But still my orders are to segregate you. You possess knowledge and skill which we require you to use now.'

'Well?'

'Well, as a former field officer of the Secret Intelligence Service, you must have a working knowledge of the diplomatic and military communications network.'

'Yes.'

'Tell me, then, do you know what an EPOC frequency is?'

'Yes.'

He remained as bland as before, though the turn of the conversation was beginning to worry him. The last time Bond had heard of EPOC frequencies was when he had had to guard against aggressive signal monitoring during a visit to Europe by the President of the United States. EPOC stood for Emergency Presidential Orders Communications. An EPOC frequency was the cleared radio frequency on which emergency messages could be sent out by the President during an official tour outside the United States.

'And what kind of signal is sent over an EPOC frequency?'

Bond paused, as though giving the matter some thought. 'Only vital military instructions. Sometimes a response to a military problem demanding the President's decision alone. Sometimes action inaugurated by him.'

'And how are these orders transmitted?'

'Usual high-speed traffic, but on a line kept permanently clear, via one of the communications satellites.'

'No, I mean the nature of the transmissions. The form they take.'

'Oh. A simple group of digits. Data, I suppose. The orders that can be given through the EPOC frequency are very limited. It's rarely used you know.'

'Quite.' Holy gave what could only be described as a knowing smile. 'Rarely used, and very limited – but with the most far-reaching consequences?'

Bond agreed. 'The President would use the EPOC frequency only on strong recommendation from his military advisers. The messages are usually concerned with rapid deployment of conventional troops and weapons . . .'

'The alteration in the Readiness State of nuclear strike capacity?'

'That's a priority, yes.'

'And tell me, would the instructions be obeyed? Immediately, I mean. Suppose the President were, for the sake of argument, in

Venice and wished both to put NATO forces on the alert and prepare his nuclear strike forces for action. Would it be done? Without consultation?'

'Quite possibly. The code for that kind of action is, in effect, a computer program. Once it's fed into the system it works. In the scenario you're suggesting, the British Prime Minister and the Commander-in-Chief NATO would consult back. But the Readiness State would continue.'

'And if the British Prime Minister and the C-in-C NATO forces were known to be with the President at the moment of transmission?'

It was very dangerous ground. Bond felt his stomach turn over. Then he remembered Rahani's words – 'No blackmail . . . no plots to kidnap the President, or hold the world to ransom . . .'

'In those circumstances the instructions would go to all local commanders automatically. They would be fed into the mainframe computers, the program would begin to run, globally, straight away. No question.' This was something more devious, more ingenious than some harebrained revolutionary plan to override the system and transmit presidential orders to raise the level of tension between the superpowers. 'But surely you know all of this.'

'Indeed I do.' There was an almost insane tranquillity in the way in which Holy answered. 'Oh, I know the minutiae. Just as I know who has access to the daily ciphers for use through the EPOC frequency, and who also has access to that frequency.'

'Tell me.' Bond gave the impression of not knowing the small print.

'Come, Mr Bond. You know as well as I do.'

'I'd rather hear it from you, sir.'

'There are only eleven ciphers that are capable of being sent via EPOC. These are seldom altered, for, as you say, they are programs, designed to be automatically set in motion while the President is out of the country. The eleventh is, incidentally, a countermand program to stop an order, returning things to the status quo. But that can be used only on a limited time scale. The frequency itself is altered at midnight every two days. Right?'

'I believe so.'

'The ciphers are carried by that omnipresent, and somewhat frightening official known as the Bag Man. Correct?'

'The system has been found reliable,' Bond agreed. 'There was a Bag Man present in JFK's entourage in Dallas. It's never been changed. He's always around – in the United States as well as when the President travels abroad. It's the penalty for having your head of state as C-in-C Armed Forces.'

'The Bag Man can part with the ciphers and EPOC frequency only to the President, or the Vice-President, should anything happen,' Holy went on. 'Should the President meet with a fatal accident overseas, the ciphers would be immediately null and void, unless the Vice-President were with him.'

'Yes.'

'So, if someone – anyone – were in possession of the EPOC frequency, and the eleven ciphers, it would be possible to relay a command which would automatically begin to run?'

For the first time since they had started talking, Bond smiled, slowly shaking his head. 'No. There is a fail safe. The EPOC frequency is a beamed satellite signal. It goes directly through one of the Defense Communications Satellite Systems, and they are very tricky little beggars. The program will run only if the satellite confirms that the signal has come directly from the area where it knows – because it has been told – the President is. You would have to be *very* close to him before you could beat the system.'

'Good.' To Bond's surprise, Jay Autem Holy looked quite happy. 'Would you be surprised to learn that we already have the eleven ciphers, the programs?'

'Nothing surprises me any more. But if you're playing games with an Emergency Presidential Order you still have to get hold of the frequency for the forty-eight hours when you plan to operate. Then you have to get close to the President, and be able to use the frequency. I'd say the last two were the hardest parts – getting near the President with the equipment needed to transmit, and obtaining the necessary frequency.'

'So who else knows the EPOC frequency – always? I'll tell you, Mr Bond. The Duty Intelligence Officer at the NATO C-in-C's Headquarters, the Duty Communications Officer at the CIA HQ Langley, the Duty Communications Officer at NSA, the corresponding senior communications officers of the US armed forces – and, Mr Bond, the senior monitoring officer at GCHQ Cheltenham. The Duty Security Officer at the British Foreign Office – who is always a member of the Secret Intelligence Service – is also in possession of the frequency. It's quite a list, when you consider that the President himself doesn't know the EPOC frequency until he has occasion to use it.'

'They're so very rarely used. Yes, as I remember it, you've got the list right – but for one other person.'

'Who?'

'The officer who controls the ciphers and frequency at the outset. Normally a communications security officer with the National Security Agency.'

'Who usually, Mr Bond, has forgotten the details within five minutes. What we shall need from you is the precise EPOC frequency on a particular day, which means we need it twenty-four hours in advance. All other details are taken care of.'

'And how do you expect me to give you the EPOC frequency?'

Jay Autem Holy gave a throaty laugh. 'You have done service as Duty Security Officer at the Foreign Office. You know the system and the routine. Someone with your background and your expertise should have no difficulty in obtaining what we require. Just put your mind to it. This is why you were the obvious candidate, Bond. Providing you're as straight as we believe you to be. There is an old proverb: when you want something from the lions, send a lion, not a man.'

'I've never heard that before.'

'No? You are the lion going to the lions. You are trusted, but if you should fail us . . . Well, we are not forgiving people, I'm afraid. Incidentally, I'm not surprised you didn't recognise the proverb. I just invented it.'

Jay Autem Holy threw back his head in a guffaw of laughter. James Bond did not think it was at all funny.

'You'll get the frequency for us, won't you, Bond?' The query came out through a series of deep breaths, as he gained control of himself. 'Think of it as your revenge. I promise you it will be used for good, and not to create havoc and disaster.'

He had no option. 'Yes, I'll do it. It's only a few numbers you want, after all.'

'That's right. You're in the numbers racket now. A few simple digits, Mr Bond.' He paused, the vivid green eyes boring into Bond's skull. 'Did you know the Soviets use almost an identical method when the General Secretary and Chairman of the Central Committee is abroad? They call it the Panic frequency – but in Russian of course.'

'You need access to this Panic frequency as well?' Bond asked, his nerves on edge.

'Oh, we already have it. You're not the only person in the numbers racket, Mr Bond. Our principals in this operation have little money to spare but they certainly have contacts. Light on cash but heavy on information. They do not trust your judgment as we do – or have I already told you that?'

'Ah, your principals, yes.' Bond turned down the corners of his mouth. 'Even though my part in all this is vital – essential – I am not allowed to know . . . ?'

'The name of our principals? I should have thought a man like you would have guessed already. A once powerful and very rich organisation, which has fallen on bad times – mainly because they lost their last two leaders in tragic circumstances. Our principals are a group who call themselves SPECTRE. The Special Executive for Counterintelligence, Terrorism, Revenge and Extortion. I rather like the revenge bit, don't you?'

14

BUNKER'S HILL

Tigerbalm and Happy, the strong-arm men in residence, cheerfully took Bond back to his room and left him, keeping up their good humoured banter the whole time.

Yet something was different, Bond knew. In his present bemused state, he could not work out what it was.

Stretching out on the bed, he looked up at the ceiling and put his mind to the current problem. It all seemed so unreal, particularly in this pleasant room with its white gloss paint and flowered wallpaper. Yet here he was, with the knowledge that downstairs a scientist had already run simulations for criminal activities and was now training people for some other, more dangerous mission using microcomputer games techniques and his own particular skills.

It was even more difficult to believe, as Jay Autem Holy had suggested, that, packaged to SPECTRE's requirements, the plan concerned military orders transmitted by the United States President. It had not surprised him to learn that SPECTRE, as principals in the matter, did not approve of Bond's recruitment. After all, they had carried on a death feud for more years than either party cared to remember.

But that was neither here nor there at this moment. Jay Autem Holy had disclosed the reason for Bond being on the payroll. Now it was up to him to be convincing.

M had been clear about the way this kind of situation should be handled. 'If they take you in – if any organisation takes you in

– then you will have to split yourself in two,' he had counselled. First, Bond should not think of any recruitment as either serious or long-term; second, he had to believe it was serious. The ultimate paradox. 'If they want you for a specialist job, you must at all costs treat it as a reality. Work it out, as they would expect of you, like a professional.'

So now, lying on the bed, with part of his mind treating the situation with grave suspicion, James Bond began to tackle the problem of how to get hold of the EPOC frequency for these people.

There was one small ray of hope. To secure that set of numbers he would have to get in touch with the outside world. It would mean communication with the Service and it was probable that contact would eventually be physical – which meant escape. What he now had to do was plot a plausible method of making the right contact to get hold of the special frequency. At the same time, he must devise a way to do this with full knowledge and co-operation from his own Service.

It took half an hour for him to concoct two possible methods, though both presupposed he would be allowed to work alone. The first plan needed Cindy Chalmer's undercover assistance, and a method of getting to his Bentley. If this were not possible, then the second plan would have to suffice, though it contained a number of imponderables, some of which could come unbuttoned with worrying ease.

He was still working out this reserve plan when he realised what was different. Once Tigerbalm and Happy left, there had been no click of key in lock.

Sliding quietly off the bed, he went over to the door and tried the handle. It opened without resistance. Was it an error or a message from the Master of Endor telling him he was free to go wherever he liked? If the latter, then Bond would have put money on it being a very limited rein. Why not put it to the test? There were plenty of reasons for trying. He had no idea what had been going on in the world lately.

The corridor took him out to a landing, the landing to the main staircase, which brought him into the hall. There, all possibility of real freedom ended. Seated near the door, dressed in jeans and a rollneck, was a young man he recognised from Erewhon. Another graduate from that alma mater lounged near the door to the laboratory stairs.

Giving each guard a friendly nod of recognition, which was returned with only a hint of suspicion in their eyes, he strolled through to the main drawing room where he had last sat with Freddie, Peter, Cindy and their hosts before dinner on the night which now seemed a hundred years ago.

The room was empty. He looked around, in the hope of spotting some newspapers. None – not even the television guides. There was a television set, however, and he strode quickly to it. The set was dead. Plugged in, switched on at the mains, but dead as a stone. The same applied to the radio tuner on the stereo system.

Nothing was coming into Endor through normal channels. Bond was sure that any other television or radio would also be inoperable, and that meant he and possibly others, had to be separated from world events. Cut off. In isolation.

He stayed downstairs for five minutes or so then returned to his room.

About an hour later Tigerbalm came to tell him they were going to have a meal shortly. 'The chief says you can join us.' He showed no feelings towards Bond, either friendly or hostile. Somewhere along the road Tigerbalm's bouncy bonhomie had been removed.

The dining room was bare of its good furniture. In place of the Jacobean table, a series of functional, military trestle tables had been set up, while the food was collected from a cloth-covered table at the side. There were soups, bread, cheese and several salad dishes. All very simple, with only mineral water to drink.

The room, however, was crowded and Bond recognised most of the faces from Erewhon. Only Tigerbalm and Happy appeared

out of their depth, heavy and sly among the sunburned, sol-
dierly young men.

'James, great to see you.' Simon stood at his elbow.

'Wondered where you'd got to.'

Bond studied the face carefully. The openness, so noticeable at
Erewhon, had become artificial. Simon's pretence told Bond far
more about the situation than all the double-talk in the world.
Whatever the plot set in motion by SPECTRE through these
people, it was already running. D minus two, three, four or five,
he reckoned. Then he drastically reduced the odds as he spotted
Tamil Rahani, seated on one side of St John-Finnes, with General
Zwingli on the other. The three men sat apart from everyone else
at a smaller table, and were being served with food by a pair of
younger soldiers. Like the others, they were dressed in uniform
olive slacks and drab green pullovers, their heads bent in deep
conversation.

For a second Bond's mind drifted off to M's surveillance team
in the village. Had they noted the comings and goings? Were
they aware of the dangerous powers gathered together in this
place?

'I said, did you rest well?' Simon was repeating.

'Rest? Oh, rest, yes.' Bond managed a smile. 'I had no alternative, Simon. You saw to that.'

'Come on, have some food.' He began piling salads and cheese
on to a plate until Bond had to stop him with a gesture of his
hand.

They sat together at the end of one of the longer tables, Simon
seeing to it that Bond had his back to the three leaders.

'Security,' said Simon with a grin, in answer to Bond's last
remark. 'You know all about security, James. Perchance to
dream, and a ride on the magic carpet. You go to sleep in a
hot dusty climate, and wake up in a quiet English village. Would
that all travel were so easy.'

'I prefer to know where I've been, and where I'm going. I like
to be aware.'

'Sure.' He took a mouthful of bread and cheese, chewing on it, sucking the juices back into his throat. Simon, Bond thought, was every inch a trained soldier. His face was the face of millions of men who marched from the Battle of Kadesh to the urban horrors of the present day.

'Hallo, the Professor's coming your way, James. Looks as if he's got orders for you.'

St John-Finnes leant over them. 'James,' his voice had a quiet, confiding tone, as though trying to calm a wayward child, 'can you spare an hour or two?'

Bond just checked himself from making a fatuous remark, nodded and rose, winking at Simon as he followed the Master of Endor, as he now thought of him, from the room. He could feel the eyes of Rahani and Zwingli on his back as they left.

There was a young man guarding the stairs down to the laboratory. He did not even signify that he had seen them, almost ostentatiously looking the other way.

'I thought I'd give you a chance to lose the American Revolution to me,' Jay Autem said as they began the descent. 'It's an easy enough simulation at this level, so we can, perhaps, talk about your plans as we fight. Yes?'

'Whatever you say.' Bond appeared noncommittal, but ran his plan for getting the EPOC frequency through his mind.

Neither Cindy nor Peter was in the main laboratory, and there had been a radical rearrangement. The largest area was now filled with collapsible wooden chairs, arranged in rows like a school assembly hall. At the far end, facing the chairs, were a large television projection screen and Jay Autem Holy's version of the Terror Twelve on a movable table.

Bond noticed two modern typing chairs and the big, chunky joystick controllers near by. A training session had obviously been going on earlier that day. The Balloon Game? Almost certainly.

They passed through into the long room with its map of the Eastern seaboard of eighteenth-century America; Boston with Bunker's Hill and Breed's Hill to the north, Dorchester Heights Jutting out to enclose the harbour, and the townships of Lexington and Concord inland. For no apparent reason, Bond recalled hearing Americans pronounce Concord with a shortened second syllable so that it sounded like Conquered. Jay Autem Holy was smiling down at the board, with its movable open rectangle, and all the games paraphernalia set at the players' places.

Bond noticed the smile and the look, and in that second saw, for all the man's brilliance, the chink in his armour revealed. His interest in strategy and tactics had become an obsession – an obsession with winning. Holy was interested only in winning. To lose was the ultimate failure. Like an over-indulged child, to win was necessary, otherwise he could not live with himself. Had he lost some internal Pentagon battle when he disappeared all those years ago? Bond wondered, steeling himself.

This fanatical Games Master was now issuing rapid instructions. Bond prepared to win the American Revolution, and so put Jay Autem Holy at a psychological disadvantage.

The rules were simple enough. Each player took a turn, which was divided into four movements: Orders, Movement, Challenge and Resolution. Some of these moves could be made in secret by marking the location of troops, or matériel, on a small duplicated map of the playing area, a pile of which rested in front of each player.

'When we transfer the whole thing on to computer there will be a more ingenious method of making the unobserved moves,' Holy told him with all the pride of a small boy showing off a collection of toy soldiers.

The playing area itself, on the grid of the large map, was marked out in hundreds of black hexagonals. Each player had counters which represented the number, strength and type of unit – black for a piece of cannon with horses and crew, green for five men, blue for ten, red for twenty, and so on. There were also counters overprinted with a horse, denoting mounted troops, and special counters to represent arms caches and the rebel leaders.

In good weather men could move five hexagonals on foot, seven on horseback, and cannon only two. These moves were restricted by bad weather, woodland or hills.

Once Orders had been noted, the player moved and then challenged, either by coming within two hexes of an enemy counter or by declaring that he had sight over five hexes, thereby revealing any hidden moves. After the Challenge came the Resolution in which various strengths, fatigue, weather, were taken into consideration, and the outcome of the Challenge would be noted, one or the other player losing troops, materiel, or the action itself.

As each turn, at the beginning, covered a time-scale of one day – and the whole episode lasted from September 1774 to June 1775 – Bond realised they could be at it for many hours.

'Once we get it on computer, the whole business becomes faster, of course,' Holy remarked as they began their Orders phase – with Bond playing the British. He remembered what Peter had told him: that his opponent almost expected the British to make the same moves – and mistakes – as they had in history.

As Bond recalled it, the garrison commander had been hamstrung by the length of time orders took to reach him from England. Had he acted decisively in the first weeks and months, this opening period could have had a very different outcome. While Independence would almost certainly have followed eventually, lives as well as face might have been saved.

Bond opened by showing patrols going out of Boston to search the surrounding countryside. He also made secret forays in order to gain control of the high ground at Bunker's and Breed's Hills, together with the Dorchester Heights, at an early stage.

He was surprised to find how much faster the game moved than he had expected.

'The fascination for me,' Holy observed as Bond took out two arms caches and around twenty revolutionaries on the Lexington road, 'is the juxtaposition of reality and fiction. But, in your former job, this must have been a constant problem.'

Bond secretly took three more cannon towards Breed's Hill, and a section of thirty men in a final move to the top of Dorchester Heights, while showing more patrols on the ground along the Boston-Concord line. 'Yes.' Be truthful, he thought, 'Yes, I have lived a fictitious life within a reality. It is the daily bread of field agents.'

'I trust you are living in reality now, friend Bond. I say that because what is being planned in this house can also change the course of history.'

Holy revealed two strong bodies of the Colonial Militia along the road, attacking the British patrols so fiercely that Bond lost almost twenty men and was forced to withdraw and regroup. Secretly, though, he still poured men, and weapons on to the dominating ground. The Battle of Bunker's Hill – if it ever came – would be completely reversed, with the British forces in a strong and dominant position, defending instead of attacking under the withering fire of the entrenched Militia.

'One hopes that any change can only be for the good, and that lives are not put at risk,' Bond said after a pause.

'Lives are always at risk.'

The Master of Endor found himself losing four caches of weapons and ammunition in a farmhouse on the far side of Lexington. He realised that Bond had also begun to move his forces on Concord. He shrugged. 'But, as for your own life, I know there is no point in threatening you with sudden death. Any threat to your person is of little importance.'

'I wouldn't say that.' Bond found himself smiling. 'We all like life. The thought of being separated from it is as good a lever as any.'

The date on the calendar easel showed them almost at the end of December, and the weather was against both sides. All either of them could do now was consolidate – openly, or by using the clandestine option. Bond decided to divide his forces, encircling the road between Lexington and Concord, while his remaining troops continued to fortify the hills and heights. Jay Autem Holy appeared to be playing a more devious game, sniping at British patrols and, Bond suspected, moving forces on to the high ground already occupied by the British. They played, turn after turn as the weather grew worse and movement was constantly restricted. Throughout this phase, the Master of Endor carried on a conversation that appeared to have little to do with the simulated battle.

'Your part in our mission . . .' he took out five of Bond's men '. . . is of exceptional importance, and you will undoubtedly have to use much fiction and illusion, to accomplish it.'

'Yes. I've been giving it a lot of thought.'

'Have you given thought to the way governments mislead their gullible peoples?'

'How do you mean?' Bond now had sizeable forces on all three sections of ground overlooking Boston.

'The obvious, of course, is the so-called balance of power. The United States does not draw attention to the fact that it is outnumbered in space by Russian satellites – not to mention things like the fractional orbital bombing system, in which the Soviets hold a monopoly of seventeen to zero.'

'The figures are there for anybody to see.' Bond would soon have to make a serious challenge from the high ground, as Colonial forces struggled upwards in increasing numbers, restricted by both the climb and the weather.

'Oh yes, but neither side makes a big thing about figures.' Holy scanned the board, brow creased. 'Except when Russia takes umbrage at the deployment of Cruise and Pershings in Europe. Even when she can more than adequately match them. But James, what is the real conspiracy here? The British government ties up many policemen controlling anti-nuclear protesters. Yet nobody says to these well-meaning people, "If it happens, brothers and sisters, it's not going to happen with the big nuclear bang, Cruise and Pershing are only for rattling. What could occur would be ten thousand times worse." They do not stop to tell the worthy ladies at Greenham Common or the marchers in London.'

'Nobody tells the protesters in the United States either.' Bond watched as his opponent edged even larger numbers of men towards the waiting British guns, and fought a small skirmish along the constant battlefront of the country between Boston and Concord.

'And yet, if it came, James, what *would* happen?'

'Your guess is as good as mine. Certainly not the big bang and the mushroom cloud. More like the bright lights and a very nasty chemical cloud.'

'Quite . . . I challenge from this hex.' Holy's arm moved out, to an area between Concord and Lexington, where British troops were now much thinner on the ground. 'No, it will be neutrons and chemicals. A lot of death, but little destruction. Then a confrontation in space, with the Soviets holding the big stick up there.'

'Unless the United States and NATO have done something to equalise things. That's what is going on, isn't it?' Why this? Bond asked himself. Why talk to me about the balance of power, and the place nuclear weapons play in that balance?

Then he recalled the sound advice always given in classes on interrogation – listen to the words, ignore the orchestration that makes the banal words seem more intelligent; the clever, soaring strings that take your mind from the cheap potency of simple, emotional ideas.

By now it was late January in the game and, at a Challenge, Bond had to reveal there were British forces ringing the far side of Concord. Jay Autem Holy started to cut them apart with his Colonial Militia, sniping across the winter landscape. Bond saw how addictive this kind of exercise could become. You could almost feel the cold and fatigue which played havoc with men's strength and fighting ability. You even heard the crack of musket fire, and saw the blood staining the dirty snow in some farmer's field.

Dr Jay Autem Holy was not really talking about the lopsided balance of power. He was talking about the need to end the whole system which controlled that balance.

'Would the world not be a better and safer place if the real strength were removed?' he asked, making another foray into the bleak Massachusetts winter scene. 'If the stings were drawn from the superpowers' tails?'

'If it were possible, yes,' Bond agreed. 'It would be better, but I doubt safer. The world's always been a dangerous place.' One more turn and he would have to declare his presence in the hills.

Holy leaned back, temporarily stopping play. 'We're involved in halting the race to the holocaust – nuclear, neutron or chemical. To you is entrusted the task of getting that EPOC frequency. Now, do you yet have a way?' As though he did not expect an answer, he played through his turn, concentrating on bringing men well into the British firing zone.

'I have the makings of a plan. It will require certain information in advance . . .'

'What kind of information?'

'When you need the frequency, I shall have to know, a little ahead of time, exactly who is the Duty Security Officer, for the night in question, at the Foreign Office . . .'

'That presents no problem. One man does the job for a whole week, yes?'

'As a rule.'

'And he is a senior officer?'

Bond spread the fingers of his right hand, making a rocking movement. 'Let's say middle management.'

'But you are likely to know him?'

'That's why I have to get a name. If you can't provide it, I shall have to telephone . . .'

'We can.'

'Then, if I know him, I shall still have to make a call. If he is unknown to me – an unlikely possibility – I'll have to think again.'

'If you know him?'

'I have a way of getting in. I should need an hour at the most in his company.' Bond prayed it would work. He had to have some communication with the outside world.

'I challenge you here.' Bond's finger hovered around the upper reaches of Breed's Hill.

'But . . .' his opponent began, then realised the trap which Bond had sprung.

A few minutes later, as he faced slaughter on the slopes of Bunker's Hill, having lost the majority of his men and arms on Dorchester Heights and Breed's Hill, Jay Autem angrily told Bond that he would have plenty of warning. 'You'll know who the officer is, that I promise you.' He watched as Bond revealed two more cannon to counter-attacking militia on the far side of the hill. 'This is the wrong way round,' he said, barely controlling his rage. 'And Bunker's Hill shouldn't happen until June. It's hardly February!'

'And this is the fiction,' Bond said. 'The reality's history – even though a great deal of history happens to be fiction too.'

He was quite pleased with his showing on this simulation, and allowed imagination to run riot. The weather for this series of turns was heavy rain, with a cold blustery wind running up from the sea. The wind raged as men and guns were locked on the barren hill, their cries lost in the cold, while the rebels still in Boston were at the mercy of British guns from Dorchester and Breed's Hill.

Then, suddenly, the storm broke. Jay Autem Holy's chest seemed to swell, and his cheeks turned from red to crimson.

'You . . . You . . . You . . .' The voice rose to a scream. 'You've beaten me! ME!' One huge hand swept the papers from his playing area, then came down in a fist. 'How dare you? How dare you even . . .'

It was an awesome rage as he spluttered, stamping his feet,

kicking the table. Awesome, and yet funny, as a child's tantrums are amusing yet distressing. He went on spluttering, blustering, out of control to the extent that Bond thought he would be physically attacked. The man was, as he had already thought, quite unhinged, with a dangerous, deep-seated madness.

Then, as suddenly as the rage had begun, it stopped. There was no dusk, no twilight, for sanity appeared to return, and he stood, looking for a brief moment like a chastened child.

'The Militia could rally yet.' The voice was small, throaty. 'But we've played too long. I have other things to do. Better things.'

He stood, as though winning or losing a game were now of little consequence to him. When he spoke again, the tone was completely normal, as if nothing unusual had taken place, quiet and conversational, making it all the more bizarre.

'The object of spending this time with you was to hear how your thoughts were shaping up – regarding your part in the operation. Tell me, if you happen to know the man on duty, how do you propose to get the frequency from him?'

Bond was amazed to see from his watch that it was eight in the evening. He began to tell Holy of the method he had prepared. When he had finished, silence stretched out – the hush in the aftermath of a battle fought with counters instead of men, and on a board and map instead of ground. As the seconds ticked by, Bond thought perhaps there had been a miscalculation. Word perfect, he sifted through his mind. Was there any really weak point? Anything that Jay Autem Holy could grab at to prove the whole idea an insubstantial fiction – which, certainly, it was.

Then the silence ended, and a laugh began to rise from the tall man's throat, the head nodding in great beaky movements, as if preparing to tear his prey apart, savaging it with that sharp bill.

'Oh yes, James Bond. I told them you were the only possible choice. If you can pull that off we'll all be happy.' He appeared to pull himself together, eyes darting around, as though he had been on the brink of an indiscretion.

The laughter subsided, and Bond was aware of movement, noises off. People were entering the main laboratory area.

'We have been down here too long,' Holy snapped. 'I took the trouble to ask Cindy to make up a tray for you. In your room. I shall eat later.'

Superman, thought Bond. He's telling me that he's a survivor. Go without food and drink for long periods.

'In the desert,' Bond said softly, 'when you were with Zwingli – after you jumped from that aeroplane – did you have to go long without food and drink?'

The green eyes went bitterly cold, all sign of normal human life ebbing from them.

'Clever, Mr Bond. How long have you known?'

Realising that he might have overplayed his hand, and not certain why he had done it, Bond said he had not been sure, but had suspected the truth from their first meeting. 'It just happened that I'd read the old file: they resurrect it from time to time, you know. I thought I knew your face the moment we met – when I came here with Freddie. During the evening, I became more convinced, but still not absolutely certain. After all, if you are Jay Autem Holy, you've been dead a long time.'

'And what if you had still been on active service, Mr Bond? Would you have gone running to your superiors? And why, incidentally, is the file resurrected regularly?'

'You know what the Colonial Militia is like,' Bond tried to inject humour into his voice. '*Your* Colonial Militia. They jump at ghosts. Spooks.'

Holy made a growling noise. 'Tamil was right. It's a pity we didn't pull you in sooner. His people tried, against my advice. You see, I did not wish to deal with yet another hostage, another woman. You had some woman with you, didn't you? Anyway, the job was bungled; you were quick and cunning.' The tense atmosphere changed yet again. There were no warnings with Holy. 'Well, I have work to do. You stand by, James. I'm glad we have you now.'

Everyone was assembling in the main laboratory, all the young bronzed soldiers from Erewhon. Bond saw that Zwingli was still in deep conversation with Tamil Rahani, as though they had not stopped since lunch.

'Just see Mr Bond up the stairs,' Holy said to Tigerbalm, giving Bond a small pat on the shoulder, as if reassuring himself that all was well.

Tigerbalm went as far as the landing, and watched as Bond walked to his room. He remembered being told that Jay Autem Holy was a genius of sorts. Was it Percy who had told him? The man obviously lived in that odd world of unreality. If he said he was dead, then that was exactly what the world should believe. Holy had been genuinely shaken by the idea that others may not be convinced. Then there was the question of Percy: 'You had some woman with you, didn't you?' Well, everyone said that Holy would not even recognise his own wife.

He opened the door, and there, for the second time since the whole intrigue had started, was Cindy Chalmer, a hard computer disk clutched in one hand, a finger to her lips. Bond closed the door. 'More greetings from Percy?' he asked softly.

15

THE BALLOON GAME

'No, this one's on me.' She saw the look in Bond's eye, and followed his gaze, for he had suddenly fallen silent, moving quietly around the room, examining every inch.

Softly she spoke again. 'It's okay, James. They have visual surveillance and all the military detection gear, but this lot don't seem to have caught up with the deadly little bug.'

'You certain?' he mouthed.

'Swept the place myself. In my first week. And I've kept abreast of all the security developments since. If they've put any sound in, I'll turn back into a virgin.'

The cruel lips didn't tilt into amusement. There was nothing to be amused about now. Even though he appeared satisfied, throughout the time they were together in the room all conversation was conducted in a low murmur. Foolish, he thought, for that would be as audible as yelling should Cindy be proved wrong.

'The Balloon Game.' She held out the hard disk to him, a small flat square, encased in plastic.

So she had got it, the program which would provide a clue – no, more than a clue – to what SPECTRE had proposed to Rahani and Holy. Stored away on the wafer-thin magnetic disk was the answer to all Bond's questions. Yet he did not move to take it from her.

'Well, don't just stand there. At least say thank you.'

He remained silent, wishing to draw her out. The trick was as old as the trade itself, practised constantly by case officers and agent handlers the world over. Remain silent and let them come to you, tell you all there is to tell. Only then should you try to fill in the gaps.

'They've got four back-up copies,' she said at last, 'and I just hope to heaven the Old Bald Eagle doesn't need to run the fourth, because this is it.'

Bond remained silent. He did not smile.

'I thought they'd buried it, locked it behind steel and sprinkled man-eating spiders in the vault.'

She stared back at Bond, who did not move.

'All five disks have been kept in the chief's safe – the one in his office that does have everything except the man-eating spiders.' Once more she held it out. 'But today it's all systems go, and they're using it all the time. As often happens Peter and I have been banished from the lab. But the guards have got used to us going up and down. I guess you beat him at his own game?'

'Yes,' Bond said flatly, as though there had been no pleasure in it.

'Heard some of it. Now perhaps you'll believe he's insane. Had one of his tantrums. I heard that as well.'

'How did you get down?'

'Looked as though I belonged. Clip-board under one arm. I just walked past the young thugs on the door. They've seen me before. You were with Bald Eagle. Like a lot of people who become paranoid about security, he has a blind spot. The safe was left open. I did a swift switch and tucked this up my shirt.'

It was all he was going to get. 'You haven't seen it run, then?'

She shook her head. Her negative gestures, he noticed, were always performed with the head tilted slightly to the right – a distinctive mannerism, a flourish, like the way some people curl the last letter of their signature, underlining the name to give it more importance. It was a habit they should have caught during training, where the mohair-suited psychiatrists note and eradicate idiosyncracies. He waited again.

'There's been no way, James. Only the inner circle have seen it, played with it – if that's the right word.'

At last Bond took the disk. 'Trained on it,' he corrected her. 'And there's little chance of us having a look-see. Where's my gear?'

'In the garage, under a pile of rubbish – tyres, old tins, tools: odds and ends. In one corner. I had to improvise, and it was better to hide it there than let them find it in the car. It's not safe by any means, so we just have to hope nobody goes rooting around.'

He seemed to give the situation a lot of thought.

'Well, I don't fancy trying to unlock this,' he touched the disk. 'What's on it is big, and I suspect dangerous. I just hope you're right – that the disk isn't missed, and that nobody goes rooting through the garage and tumbles over my hoard of electronics.'

'So what good's it going to do? You want me to try and get it out?'

Bond went over to the window, where the chintz curtains had been drawn. The promised supper tray was on a table near by, and he noticed it had been set for two – prawns in little glasses, cold chicken and tongue, salads, bread rolls, a bottle of wine. Did anybody get hot food at Endor when the heat was on? he wondered. He still clutched the disk in his hand. Better if he kept it close. Yet there were so few hiding places. In the end, he banked on there being no search, walked over to the wardrobe and pushed it among his clothes. The whole process seemed to take several minutes of silence.

'There are friends,' he confided at last. 'Quite near. I would have thought that by now . . . No, you don't move from the house. Nobody tries to get out except me.' Bond turned, and dropped quietly into a chair, signalling she should also sit. He nodded towards the wardrobe. 'We're not taking any risks, not with that. It's like a time bomb.'

'We just sit, and wait until the cavalry arrive?' Cindy was

perched on the end of the bed, her skirt riding up to show a slice of smooth, tantalising thigh.

'Something like that.' Bond was trying to reckon how much time they might have; whether the team with their cameras, log books and directional microphones had advised M that something important was happening at Endor. Would M let them sweat it out? Possibly. The cautious, diplomatic intriguer had waited before, almost until the last moment.

'I want an educated guess from you, Cindy. You've been here before – I mean when they've prepared for some caper.'

She had been at Endor before, when the hard men had come and spent hours training down in the converted cellars.

'This is the biggest gathering yet?'

Since she had been here, it was.

'In your estimation, Cindy, what's the timing? How long have we got before things start to roll?' In his mind the question was really, how long have *I* got before they ask me to filch the EPOC frequency?

'It can only be a guess, but I'd say forty-eight hours maximum.'

'And your little playmate, Peter?'

She sprang to Peter's defence like a sister, often at loggerheads with her brother, but always ready to stand up for him. 'Peter's okay. He's a brilliant worker, dedicated . . .'

'Would you trust him? Really trust him, when the chips are down, as they say?'

She gnawed her upper lip. 'Only in a real emergency. Nothing against him. He can't stand St John-Finnes or Dazzle. He's been looking for a different job. Says this place is too claustrophobic for him.'

'I expect it'll be even more claustrophobic soon,' Bond said. 'I'd say you, Peter and myself are destined for oblivion – particularly you and Peter. Anybody who isn't completely in their confidence.'

Once more he fell silent, his mind slicing through every

morsel of information. Jay Autem Holy had indicated that SPECTRE's current ploy was destined to change history. Afterwards, they would not want anybody around who could name names or draw faces. Certainly not in the immediate wake of whatever they planned.

'My car,' he snapped suddenly.

'The Bentley? Yes?'

'You took my gear from the boot. How?'

'It was just before the present crowd arrived. I had been through the kitchens and spotted a whole lot of food being loaded into the two big deep freezes. I also heard Old Bald Eagle on the telephone. I knew they were bringing you back. What did happen by the way? They said you were in hospital . . .'

Bond brusquely told her to get on with it.

She knew the car had been driven back and put into the garage, and she wondered about the micro and drives he had used in the hotel. The Bentley's keys were left in a security cabinet where they kept all the car keys. She had been in and out of that one since she first arrived – and she chose her moment.

'It was a risk, but I only had the keys out for five minutes. Everyone was busy, so I took the keys, unloaded the boot, and stashed the stuff in the garage. It's not really safe, but it seemed to be the only way. Bad enough doing that, and far too risky to attempt getting it any further away.'

'And the car itself? Have they done anything with it? Gone over it?'

She gave her angled negative head shake. 'No time. Not enough troops either. Everyone's been up to their eyes here.'

'The keys?'

'Jason will have them.'

'And it's still there? In the garage?'

'Far as I know. Why?'

'Can we . . . ?'

'Forget it, James. There's no way we can drive out of here in one piece.'

'I hope to be going officially. But if they haven't messed about with it, I wouldn't mind spending fifteen minutes in that car now. Possible?'

'The keys? How? Lord, I don't . . .'

'Don't worry about keys. Just tell me, Cindy, can we get into the garage?'

'Well, I can.' She explained that her room had a window looking out on the garage roof. 'You just drop down, and there's a skylight. Opens upwards. No problem.'

'And security?'

'Damn. Yes, they've got a couple of young guys out front.'

She explained the layout. The garage itself held four cars, and was, in effect, an extension to the north end of the house. Her room was on the corner, just above the flat roof, one window looking down on the garage, two more to the front.

'And these guards? They're out front? Specifically watching the garage?'

'Just general duties. Keeping an eye on the north end. If we could . . . Wait a minute. If my curtains aren't drawn they can see straight up into my room. I caught one lot at it last night. They just move a shade further down the drive and they have a good view. How would it be if I gave them a peep show?'

Bond smiled for the first time. 'Well, I'd appreciate it.'

Cindy leaned back on the bed. 'You, James, you male chauvinist pig, have the opportunity to appreciate it any time you want. That's an offer.'

'I'd love to take you up on it, Cindy. But we have work to do. Let's see how good they've been with my luggage.'

He went over to the weekend case and dumped it on the bed beside the girl, then knelt to examine the locks. After a few seconds he nodded and took out the black gunmetal pen clipped inside his pullover, unscrewing the wrong end to reveal a tiny set of miniature screwdriver heads. These were threaded at their blunt ends, the threads matching a small hole in the pen's cap.

'No traveller should be without one,' Bond said. He smiled and selected one of the drivers, screwing it into place.

Carefully he began to remove the tiny screws around the right lock of his case. They turned easily, the lock coming off in one piece to reveal a small oblong cavity containing one spare set of keys for the Mulsanne Turbo, which he slipped into his pocket before replacing the lock and putting away the miniature tool kit.

The plans for Cindy's diversion and Bond's crawl from her window were quickly arranged.

'The diversion's no problem,' she said, lowering her eyelids. 'I've got exceptional quality tart's stuff on under the skirt.' She gave a little pout. 'I thought I might even turn you on.'

She described her room, suggesting that she should enter in the dark, open the side window and pull those curtains before switching the light on. 'I'll be able to see exactly where the guards have placed themselves. You'll have to crawl to the side window on your belly.'

'How long can you . . . well, tantalise them?'

If she performed the full act, Cindy said, putting on a throaty voice, she could keep them more or less happy for about half an hour. 'To be on the safe side, I guess you'd better reckon on ten minutes, give or take five.'

He gave her a look usually reserved for the more cheeky jumper and pearls set at the Regent's Park Headquarters, checked the ASP, and said the sooner they got on with it the better. Bond knew that, if Holy's men had not yet tampered with the car, it would certainly be given a going over before they let him out – if they let him out.

Nobody appeared to be stirring in the house. While tiptoeing across the landing, they saw men still lounging in the hall, but the rest was quiet, and the corridor leading to Cindy's room at the far end of the house was in darkness. Her smooth palm touched his, their fingers interlocking for a moment as she guided him towards her door.

She was young, supple, very attractive and obviously available – to him at least. For a second he wondered, not for the first time, how genuine she was. But the chance to doubt had long since passed. There was nobody else to trust.

Cindy opened her door, whispering, 'Okay, down boy.' He dropped on to his stomach, beginning to wriggle his way across the floor. Cindy was humming to herself and interspersing the low, tuneful, bluesy sound with soft comments.

'Nobody at the side . . . I'm closing the curtains . . . okay, going to the front windows . . . Yes, they're down there . . . Right, James, get cracking, I'm putting the lights on . . .' And on they flooded, with Bond halfway across the floor, moving fast towards the window, where the curtains billowed and sighed like a sail.

As he reached it, he saw her out of the corner of his eye, standing near the far front window, hands to her shirt, swaying slightly as she sang softly:

He shakes my ashes, freezes my griddle,
Churns my butter, stokes my pillow
My man is such a handyman

He threads my needle, gleans my wheat,
Heats my heater, chops my meat,
My man is such a handyman.

The last words were barely distinguishable to Bond, who was already out of the window, dropping silently on to the garage roof. He had a copy of 'Queen' Victoria Spivey's *Handyman*, recorded in the 1920s, so he knew what that was all about.

Flat against the roof, his body pressing down as if to merge with the lead surface, Bond lay silent, letting his eyes adjust to the darkness. Then he froze, hearing first the sound of feet on gravel, then the voices. There were, as Cindy had said, two of them, speaking in heavily accented English. One made a hushing sound.

'What?'

'The roof. Didn't you hear it?'

'What?'

'Sounded like someone on the garage roof . . .'

Bond willed his body into the flat surface, pressing down, his head turned away, pulses thudding in his ears.

'On the roof? No.'

'Move back. Take a look. You know what he said – no second chances.'

The sound of feet on the gravel again.

'I can't see any . . .'

'You think we should go and . . .'

Bond's hand inched towards the ASP.

'There's nobody there. Might have been a cat . . . Hey, Hans, look at that.' The scuffle of feet could be heard moving back off the gravel.

Bond turned his head, and saw the clear silhouettes of the two guards below, in front of the house. They were close to one another, looking up like a pair of astronomers studying a new planet, eyes fixed on the windows, out of sight to his right.

Carefully he started to move towards the centre of the roof, where he knew the skylight lay. Then, suddenly, he dropped flat again as the guards also moved – his own breathing sounding so loud that it must draw them to him. But the two men were now backing away from the house, heads tilted, trying to get a better view of what was happening just inside Cindy's lighted open window.

Again Bond edged forward, going as fast as safety would allow, conscious of each minute slipping away.

Though probably less than a minute, it seemed to take an eternity to reach the skylight, which moved at his first touch. Very gently he slid it back, staring down into the darkness below.

They had made it easier for him by parking the white Mercedes directly underneath. One swing and he was down, feet on the car's roof, head less than a foot below the edge of the skylight.

Crouched there, Bond slipped the ASP from its holster. If they had put a man inside the garage, plans might just have to change. Once more he waited, stock still, letting his eyes adjust to the darkness. No sound could be heard but the beating of his own heart. The long outline of the Mulsanne could just be made out parked to his right.

He dropped to the floor, padded around the rear of the Mercedes, one hand still grasping the ASP, the other now clutching the keys to the Bentley.

The lock thumped open, and there was that solid, satisfying sound as the catch gave way to his thumb and the heavy door swung back.

The Bentley's interior came alive with light, and he slid into the driving seat, leaving the door open as he checked the connections around the Super 1000 long-range telephone, which Communications Control Systems had provided for the electronics wizards at Rolls-Royce to wire in. Closing the door, he picked up the handset, letting out a breath of relief as the small pin of red light came on to show the telephone was active. His main fear had been that Holy's men had cut the connections. Now, all he could do was pray that nobody was monitoring the closed waveband.

Quickly he punched out the number, and, before the distant end had time to say 'Transworld Exports,' he rasped out, 'Predator! Confuse!' hitting the small blue scramble button as he said it, then counting to twenty, waiting for the distant to come up again.

'Confused!' the voice of the Duty Officer at the Regent's Park Headquarters said clearly.

'I say this once only. Predator, emergency . . .' and Bond launched into a fast two-minute message which he hoped would be clearly intelligible if Jay Autem Holy really intended to send him out from Endor to steal the United States EPOC frequency within the next few days.

Putting the telephone back into its cradle between the seats, he retrieved the ASP which had rested above the polished wooden dashboard only inches from his hand, and returned it to his holster.

Now he had to get back to Cindy's room as fast as possible. The thought of the girl slowly stripping, singing to herself, was highly erotic in his heightened state of mind, bringing the picture of Percy Proud to him quickly, as though she were very close. A trick of the subconscious he decided, closing the Bentley's door as quietly as its weight allowed and locking the car.

The interior lights remained on for a few seconds, then the garage was once more consigned to darkness. He turned, to head back to the Mercedes, when a sharp double metallic click brought him to a halt.

There was an old game – remembered from his training back in the Second World War – which they still played in the school. You sat in darkness while tapes of noises were run. The object was to identify each noise. Often they ran the distinctive cocking action of an automatic pistol with the sounds of door handles, toys, even metal snap fastenings. The sharp double click which he heard now came from the far side of the Mercedes, and Bond would know it anywhere. It was that of an automatic pistol being cocked.

He had the ASP in his hand again, like a master conjurer producing a wand from mid-air. But as the gun came up, a spotlight flashed on and a very familiar voice spoke softly.

'Put that nasty thing away, dear. It's not really worth it, and neither of us wants to get hurt, do we?'

16

EPOC

Bond could see him quite clearly, outlined against the lighter colouring of the wall. In a fraction of a second, his brain and body calculated the situation and made a decision.

Normally, with all his training, and the long built-in reflexes, Bond would have taken him out with one shot, probably straight from the hip. But several factors were weighed in an instant and stayed his hand.

The voice was not aggressive, indicating room for negotiation; the words had been plain, simple and to the point – '. . . neither of us wants to get hurt, do we?' More important, there was no silencer fitted to the ASP. A shot from either side would bring Holy's people into the garage. Bond reckoned that Peter was as anxious as he was himself to keep the wolves at bay.

'Okay, Peter. What's the score?'

As Peter Amadeus came closer, Bond sensed more than saw that the small pistol, just visible, held away from the body, was waving around like a tree in a gale. The precise little man was clearly very nervous.

'The score, Mr Bond, is that I want out. And as far away from here as possible. I gathered from your conversation that you're thinking of going as well.'

'I'm going when I'm told – by your boss. Does he know you're out, by the way?'

'If the gods happen to be on my side, nobody will notice. If the hue and cry is raised, I just pray they won't come looking here.'

'Peter, you won't get out at all unless I go back the way I came pretty damned quickly. Wouldn't it be better for you to stay put?'

The pistol sagged in Amadeus's hand, and his voice edged one more note towards hysteria. 'I can't, Bond! I can't do it. The place, those people – particularly Finnes – terrify me. I just can't stay in the house any longer!'

'Right,' said Bond soothingly, hoping the young man's voice would not rise too high. 'If we can think of a way, would you help? Give evidence if necessary?'

'I've got the best evidence in the world,' he said in a calmer voice. 'I've seen the Balloon Game run. I know what it's about, and that's enough to terrify any large-size policeman, let alone me.'

'What's in it? Tell me.'

'It's my only ace. You get me out and I'll give any help you might need. Is that a deal?'

'I can't promise.' Bond was acutely aware that time was slipping by. Cindy would not be able to distract the two guards much longer. He told Peter to put the gun away. 'If they're letting me out to do a bit of their dirty work, it's pretty certain they'll go through the Bentley with the finest of toothcombs. You've also got to realise that your absence puts a lot of people at risk.'

'I know, but . . .'

'Okay, it's done now. Listen, and listen carefully . . .' As quickly as he could, Bond told Amadeus the best way to hide under the other cars in the garage. Then he pressed the keys into the young man's hand. 'You use these only after they've played around with the Bentley. It's a risk. Anything could happen, and I haven't any assurance they'll let me go in my own car. One other thing. If you're found here, you get no help. I completely deny having anything to do with you. Right?'

Bond told Amadeus he should hide in the boot after the car had been examined – 'For all I know they'll send one of their people with me, armed to the teeth.' Then Bond gave him a final instruction should all else fail, or if Bond himself were prevented from going. He patted the little programmer's shoulder, wishing him luck, then climbed back on to the roof of the Mercedes and hauled himself up through the skylight.

Lying on the flat roof in the chill night air, pressed hard against the lead, he realised that Cindy had exhausted her repertoire. The guards were very close, just below the garage roof. He could hear them muttering, commenting on what they had seen: all the usual soldiers' innuendoes.

He lay tense, listening, for about five minutes, until they moved away, following their routine pattern, covering the front of the house from all angles.

It took a further ten minutes for Bond to snake his way back to the window. After each move he stopped, lying still, ears strained for sounds of the returning guards, who passed under the garage twice during his uncomfortable crawl. At last he negotiated the sill, climbing back into Cindy's room.

'You took your time.'

She was stretched out on the bed, her dark body glistening, the gorgeous long legs moving as she rubbed thigh against thigh. Cindy was quite naked, and Bond, with the tension released, went to her.

'Thank you. I've done all I can . . .' He was going to say something about Amadeus, but changed his mind; sufficient unto the day. Cindy lifted her arms to his shoulders, and Bond found himself with no power to resist.

Only once, as he entered her, did Percy's face and body flash before him – a picture so vivid that he thought he could smell her scent on Cindy.

It was almost dawn when he crept back to his own room. The house was still silent, as though sleeping in preparation for action. He ate some of the food, threw the rest down the lavatory and flushed it three times to clear it away. Only when that was done did Bond lie down on his own bed, still fully dressed, and drop into a refreshing sleep.

At the first noise he was awake, his right hand going for the ASP.

It was Cindy, looking as though even hard-boiled sweets would dissolve at the touch of her tongue. She carried a breakfast tray and was followed by Tigerbalm, who produced his inane grin, saying that Professor St John-Finnes wished to see him at noon. 'That's midday sharp,' he added. 'I'll come and fetch yer.'

'Please do.' He moved on the bed, but Cindy was already halfway out of the door.

'Cindy,' he called.

She did not even look back. 'Have a nice day' was flung sharply over her shoulder.

Bond shrugged, a little worried, and then began to help himself to black coffee and toast. It was ten-thirty by his watch. By eleven forty-five he was showered, shaved and changed, feeling better than the day before, and reflecting that even M could not leave it much longer before making a move against Endor.

At three minutes to twelve, Tigerbalm reappeared. They went downstairs to the rear of the house, where Jay Autem Holy was waiting for him in a small room Bond had never seen before.

There was a table, two chairs and a telephone; no pictures, windows or any other furnishing. The room was lit by two long neon strips, and Bond saw immediately that the chairs and table were bolted to the floor. It was familiar ground: an interrogation room.

'Come in, friend Bond.'

The head came up in a swooping movement, the green eyes piercing, hostile as laser gun sights. He told Tigerbalm to leave, motioning for Bond to sit down. Holy wasted no time.

'The plan you outlined to me – the way to get your eyes on the current EPOC frequency . . .'

'Yes.'

'It is imperative that we have the frequency which comes into operation at midnight tonight, covering the next two days.'

'I can get it, but . . .'

'We'll do without any buts, James. SPECTRE are still most unhappy about using you. They have sent a message, which I am to give you, alone.'

Bond waited. There was a pause of a few seconds.

'Those who speak for SPECTRE say that you already know they are not squeamish. They also say that it is useless for us to threaten you with death or anything else, if you do not carry out orders to the letter.' He gave the ghost of a smile. 'I happen to believe that you're with us all the way. If you're doubling, then I'd have to admit you've fooled me. However, just so that we all know where we stand, I am to tell you the worst that can happen.'

Again Bond did not reply, or allow any change in his expression.

'The operation to which we are all now committed has peaceful aims, I must stress this. True, it will alter history. Certainly it will bring about some chaos. There will undoubtedly be resistance from reactionaries. But the change will come, and with it Peace.' He made it plain, by his tone that the word was given a capital P.

'So?'

'So, the EPOC frequency is a prerequisite to SPECTRE's plan for the Peaceful solution. If all goes well, there will be little or no bloodshed. If anyone is hurt or killed, it will be the fault of those trying to make a stand against the inevitable.'

Holy clasped his hands together gently and placed them on the table in a gesture of open and frank paternal counselling.

'What I am instructed to tell you is that, should you fail us, or try any tricks to foil what cannot be foiled, the operation will still go ahead, but the Peaceful solution will have to be abandoned. Without the EPOC frequency there is one way only – the way of horror, terror and the ultimate holocaust.'

'I . . .' Bond began, but was stopped short by Holy's glare.

'They wish me to make it clear to you that, should you be tempted to cut and run, not provide the frequency, or – worse – try to alter it, then the blood and deaths of millions will be on your head, and yours alone. They are not bluffing, James. We have worked for them, and they terrify me.'

'Do they terrify General Zwingli as well?'

'He is a tough old bird,' Holy said, more relaxed. 'A tough but disillusioned old bird. But, yes, they also frighten him.' He spread his hands on the table, near the telephone, palms downwards. 'Joe Zwingli lost all faith in his country roughly at the time that I too came to the conclusion that the United States had become a degenerate, self-serving nation, led by corrupt men. I deduced that America – like Britain – could never be altered from the inside. It had to be done from without. Together we dreamed up the idea of disappearing, working for a truly democratic society, and world peace, from the obscurity of . . . what shall I call it? . . . the obscurity of the grave?'

'How about the obscurity of a whited sepulchre?' Too late, Bond checked his impulse to be less than friendly with the devious doctor.

The green eyes hardened, diamonds reflecting light. 'Not worthy, James. Not if you're with us.'

'I was thinking it was what the world might say.'

'The world will be a very different place within the next forty-eight hours. Few will be concerned with what I did. Many will look with hope to what I have done.'

Bond swerved back to the matter in hand. 'So I go tonight – if you've decided my idea's the best.'

'You go tonight, and you set things in motion before you go. The Duty Security Officer's name is Denton – Anthony Denton.'

'Good.'

'You know him?'

Bond knew Tony Denton well. They had attended courses together in the past, and, a few years ago, had been on a bring-'em-back-alive trip to secure a defector who had walked into the Embassy in Helsinki. Yes, he knew good old Tony Denton, though it would make no difference at all if his instructions had been taken to heart at the Regent's Park Headquarters.

'He goes on duty at six in the evening, I understand,' Holy prompted.

Bond said that certainly used to be the old routine. Holy suggested he should make the telephone call at about six-thirty. 'In the meantime, I think you'd better take some rest. If you do the job properly, as you must, for the sake of your own peace of mind, not to mention the millions who are unknowingly staking their lives on you, we can all look to a brighter future – to those broad, sunlit uplands of which a great statesman once spoke.'

'I go in my own car.' He was not asking but telling Holy.

'If you insist. I shall have to have the telephone disconnected, but you'll not object to that.'

'Just leave me an engine and a complete set of wheels.'

Holy allowed himself the ghost of a smile. Then the face hardened again.

'James . . .'

Bond knew suddenly that he was going to say something unpleasant.

'James, I'm giving you the benefit of the doubt. I understand the nubile Miss Chalmer was in your room last night. Come to that, you were in hers until the early hours. I must ask you, did Cindy Chalmer give you anything? Or try to pass something to you?'

'I trust not . . .' then he realised this was not the time for facetious remarks. 'No. Nothing. Should she have?'

Holy stared at the table. 'She says not. Idiot girl. Sometime yesterday she removed what she imagined to be a rather important computer program from the laboratory. She's shown signs of wilfulness before now, so I set a small trap for her. The program she stole was rubbish, quite worthless. She says that you knew nothing of her action, and I'm inclined to believe her. But the fact remains that she hid the disk among your clothes – where, James, it has been found. Cindy made quite a speech about it. She seems to think that we're – as she puts it – up to no good. So, she took the disk as some kind of evidence and hid it in your room until she could think of a way to use it against me.' He became hesitant. 'We've kept it in the family, James – by which I mean that we've not let it go beyond Dazzle and myself. My partners, Rahani and Zwingli, could become alarmed, might even pass it on to the representatives of SPECTRE. I don't think we'd want that, not a domestic thing. None of their business.'

So, thought Bond, as serious a matter as stealing even a dummy back-up program of the Balloon Game – on which, he presumed, the whole operation for SPECTRE was based – could be overlooked and kept 'in the family'. It was an interesting turn of events. What it did show was that Jay Autem Holy lived in terror of SPECTRE, and that was a piece of deduction which may well be put to valuable use later.

'Cindy?' Bond mused. 'What . . . ?'

'Will happen to her? She is regarded as one of my family. She will be disciplined, like a child, and kept under lock and key. Dazzle is seeing to it.'

'I haven't set eyes on your wife recently.'

'No, she prefers to remain in the background, but she has certain tasks to perform, tasks necessary to success. What I really wish to ask of you, James, is that we keep this business about Miss Chalmer to ourselves. Keep it as a personal matter. I mean, we don't mention it to anybody. Personal, between us, eh?'

'It's personal enough already.' Bond clamped his mouth shut. What else was there to say?

Tigerbalm came for him shortly after six o'clock. They had not locked him in, though food was served on a tray, brought up by a young Arab. Tigerbalm was very polite.

They went to the same room as before, with its bolted-down table and chairs. The only difference this time was that a tape recorder, with a separate set of earphones, had been hooked up to the telephone.

'It's time, then.'

Holy was not alone. Tamil Rahani stood beside him, while the large, craggy face of General Zwingli peered out from behind them.

'I can't promise this part will work.' Bond's voice was flat and calm. So calm that it appeared to activate something deep within General Zwingli, who pushed his way through his partners, sticking out a leathery hand.

'We haven't met, Commander Bond.' The voice had a slightly Texan tang to it. 'My name's Joe Zwingli, and I just want to wish you luck, son. Get in there and *make* it happen for us. It's in a great cause – to put your country and mine back on their feet; give them some new order in the midst of their present chaos.'

Bond did not want to disillusion the man. But a scheme of SPECTRE's that was not for their good alone, he reckoned, would never see the light of day.

He played it to the hilt. 'I'll do what I can, sir.'

Then he sat down and waited for Holy to set the tape monitor, put on the headphones and indicate they were ready.

He picked up the handset and punched out the digits to access the small complex where the SIS Duty Security Officer to the Foreign Office spent his twelve-hour watches, together with specialist teleprinter, cipher, radio and computer operators. Two shifts a day, twelve hours apiece.

The number which Bond had in fact punched was a screened telephone number known only to the field officers of his Service. It was also manned day and night, and paraded many identities, depending upon what operations were being run. That night it was a Chinese Laundry based in Soho, a radio cab firm, a French restaurant, and – if the need arose – the Foreign Office Duty Security Officer's direct line. For that purpose it had been alerted

tor special action ever since Bond's radiophone call from the
Bentley on the previous evening. If the call came, it would be
passed to one person only. The telephone rang four times before
anyone picked it up. 'Hallo?' The voice was flat, disguised for
safety.

'Tony Denton – the DO please.'

'Who wants him?'

'Predator.'

'Hang on please.'

Bond saw Holy give a wry smile, for when outlining his plan,
he had refused to give the cryptonym he had used as a member
of the Service. Apparently Jay Autem Holy thought this one very
apt.

They waited while the call was being switched through to Bill
Tanner, and it was his old friend Tanner's voice which next
came on to the line.

'Denton. I thought you were out, Predator. This is an irregular
call. I'm afraid I have to terminate.'

'Tony! Wait!' Bond hunched over the table. 'This is priority.
Yes, I'm out – as far as anyone can be out – but I have something
vital to the Service. But *really* vital.'

'Go on.' The voice at the other end sounded doubtful.

'Not on the telephone. Not safe. You're the only person I
could think of. I must see you. I have to see you. Imperative,
Tony. Consul.'

Bond used the standard cipher word for extreme emergency.
At the far end there was a fractional pause.

'When?'

'Tonight. Before midnight. I can get to you, I think. Please,
Tony, give me the all clear.'

Again there was a long pause. 'If this isn't straight I'll see you
in West End Central by morning, charged under the Official
Secrets Act. As quickly as you can. I'll clear you. Right?'

'Be with you before midnight.'

Bond sounded relieved, but the line was closed long before he took the handset from his ear.

'First hurdle.' Holy jabbed down on the recorder's stop button. 'Now, you have to be convincing when you get there.'

'So far, it's playing to packed houses.' Tamil Rahani sounded pleased. 'The dispatch rider brings the frequency up from Cheltenham at around eleven forty-five?'

'If the US President is away from his own country, yes.' Bond held the man's eyes, trying to discern his state of mind.

Rahani laughed. 'Oh, he's out of the country. No doubt about that, Commander Bond. No doubt at all.'

'If you leave here at nine forty-five you should make it with time to spare.' Holy removed his headset. 'We'll be with you all the way, James. All the way.'

17

DOWN ESCALATOR

The metal forests of antennae which rise above the massive pile of government buildings running from Downing Street along Whitehall and Parliament Street, conjure up thoughts of communications flying through the night; of telephones waking ministers, calling them to deal with some important crisis; or the fabled telegrams crossing the airwaves from distant embassies.

In fact, only open messages run into those government offices. Sensitive signals and urgent messages are usually routed through the GCHQ complex outside Cheltenham, or one of its many satellites. From Cheltenham they are passed to the mysterious building known as Century House, or to the Regent's Park Head-quarters. Ciphers for the Foreign Office go only then, not to Whitehall and Parliament Street, but to an unimposing, narrow, four-storey house off Northumberland Avenue. They are sent by a variety of methods ranging from the humble dispatch rider to teleprinter by land-line, or even through a closed telephone circuit, often linked to a computer modem programmed for de-ciphering.

If the romantically minded were to imagine that someone with the title of Duty Security Officer, Foreign Office, prowls the great corridors of power with flashlight and uniformed accomplices, they would be wrong. The DSOFO does not prowl. He sits in the house off Northumberland Avenue, and his job is to ensure that all ciphers for Foreign Office remain secure and get to the right person. He also deals with a whole mass of restricted information concerning communications from abroad, both from British sources, and from those of foreign powers. Leaders of friendly foreign powers, in particular, look for assistance from the Foreign Office. They usually find it with the DSOFO.

It was to the little-noticed turning off Northumberland Avenue that James Bond was now heading in the Mulsanne Turbo.

They had taken him out to the garage shortly after nine-thirty, made sure he had money, credit cards, his ASP, and petrol in the tank. Holy, Rahani and Zwingli had, in turn, clasped his hand, Zwingli muttering, 'Good to have you on the team,' and promptly at nine forty-five the Bentley had eased its bulk on to the gravel turning circle, flashed its lights once, and swept on its stately way, up the drive and on to the road to Banbury.

From Banbury, Bond followed the route they had ordered him to take – straight to the M4 motorway, and so into London.

He did not spot any shadows, but had no doubt that they would be there. It did not worry him. The street where he would finally stop would be cleared of all but authorised vehicles so there was little chance of him being observed once the car had been parked.

Risking the wrath of police patrols, Bond made the journey at high speed. From numerous telltale signs and bumps he was certain Peter Amadeus had managed to let himself into the boot. The little programmer would, by now, be suffering considerable discomfort. Bond stopped once, at the service station near Heathrow Airport, to fill the tank. There he was able to let a little air into the boot and to satisfy himself that Amadeus was indeed alive and well. In a whisper, he explained that release just then was impossible, but it would not be long now.

Less than forty minutes later, Amadeus was freed, speechless and stiff from the cramped ride, but all the same duly grateful.

'Well, this is where you show your gratitude.' Bond took his arm firmly, leading him towards the lighted doorway of the terraced house.

Swing doors opened on to a marble-tiled hallway with a lift which took them to the second floor and a minuscule landing, watched over by a muscular government messenger, who half rose from his desk to ask what they required.

'Predator,' Bond snapped at him. 'Tell them, Predator and friend.' He did not smile.

Less than a minute later, they were led quickly through a passage and into a larger room. The red velvet curtains were drawn. A portrait of the Queen hung over the Adam fireplace and another of Winston Churchill adorned the opposite wall. A long gleaming boardroom table occupied a large portion of the available space.

Six faces turned as one. M was at the head with Bill Tanner on his right and another officer Bond recognised to the left. Major Boothroyd, the Armourer, Head of Q Section, sat to Tanner's right with Lady Freddie Fortune next to him.

Bond did not have time to be surprised at Freddie's presence, for the sixth member of the reception committee left her chair almost at a run.

'James, darling. Oh, it's so good to see you.'

Percy Proud, oblivious to the officialdom, held him close, as though she would never let go again.

'Commander Bond! Miss Proud!' M was genuinely embarrassed. 'I, er, think we have important work to do.'

He detached himself from Percy, acknowledged the others, and introduced Peter. 'I think Dr Amadeus will be able to contribute.' Bond kept glancing suspiciously at Freddie Fortune – so often that M finally said, 'Lady Freddie's been on the team for some years. Done good work, infiltrating. Sound woman, 007. Very deep cover. Forget you've ever seen her here.'

Bond caught Freddie's steady gaze, returning it with a sardonic smile and cocked eyebrow. Then, M drew the conference to order.

'I trust you've gone into Endor, sir . . .' Bond started.

'Yes, 007. Yes, we went in about an hour after you drove out, but the birds had flown. I don't think many were left when you departed. The rest have vanished into thin air. Bag and baggage. We thought you could tell us . . .'

'I'm instructed to return there, by the same route as I came.' Bond recalled the deserted feel of the place that morning, and the fact that he had seen only Cindy and the Arab first thing, and Tigerbalm, Holy, Rahani and Zwingli later.

'The cars were there.' He felt it was a lame comment. 'Three of them, still in the garage.'

'Two when our people arrived.' The officer Bond recognised but could not name was obviously running liaison.

'How about my girl? How about Cindy?' Percy touched his sleeve, and Bond could not meet her eyes.

'I'm not certain. She was a great deal of help, last night. Even tried to steal a copy of their main program – the simulation of whatever they're doing.' He turned to M. 'It's on SPECTRE's instructions, this business, sir, did you know?'

'Is it, indeed?' M could administer the iceberg treatment when he had a mind to. 'That villainous outfit is on the warpath again, eh?'

'You still haven't told me about Cindy.' Percy had her hand tightly on his arm now.

'Just don't know, Percy. No idea.' He told her about the previous night, leaving out all that happened after he got back to her room, but repeating the conversation with Holy in the morning.

'So we have no ideas about this simulation?' M sucked at his pipe.

'If I could have a word.' They all turned towards Amadeus. 'I've seen the simulation running. It was a couple of weeks ago. The wee small hours. Couldn't sleep. I went down to the laboratory, and Jason was in what we call the War Room – Mr Bond knows: it's at the far end. Jason was engrossed. Just didn't hear me.' He passed a hand across his forehead. 'That was before all those great oafs – gun-happy boys – turned up. Before I got nervous about being there.'

M looked uncomfortable, spluttering over his pipe.

'Well, thinks I, have a look, Pete. See what the crooks are after next. They refer to it as the Balloon . . .'

'The Balloon Game, yes,' Bond interrupted.

'I've seen it and you haven't. I have the floor, Mr Bond, please.' He looked around him revelling in the attention he was getting. 'As I was saying, they call it the Balloon Game, but it's to do with something they've named Operation Down Escalator.'

M's brow creased as he repeated the words under his breath.

'The simulation . . .' Amadeus raised his voice '. . . appears to be set in a commercial airport. Not large. I didn't recognise it, but that's nothing to go by. The scenario begins in an office complex just to the left of the main terminal building. There's a lot of stuff with cars, and positioning men. As far as I could see, the idea was to lift one man.'

'Lift?' M enquired.

'Kidnap, sir,' explained Bond.

Amadeus shot them a glance, then scowled, letting them know he did not like being interrupted. 'They lift this chap, and there's a lot of changing around in cars – you know, he's taken to one point, then switched to another car. Then the location alters to a smaller field – an airfield. It's tiny, with a mini control tower and one main building, a hangar, and guess what? An airship.'

'Airship?' Bond repeated in surprise.

'Hence Balloon Game. They get on to this field using the man they've lifted. It does appear to be terribly clever – there are three cars, twelve men, and the hostage, if that's what he is. Result? They take over the whole shooting match. There is a final scenario, and that's to do with flying the airship somewhere. It got very technical and . . .'

'Chief-of-Staff,' M almost shouted. 'Go and check it out. We know the thing's there, because it's on the itinerary. Saw it myself. They cleared it with the President's people, the Prime Minister and the Russians. Doing a sort of fly-past tomorrow morning.'

Bill Tanner was out of the room before he finished.

Bond looked at his chief, the questions clear on his face. 'Sir, I haven't seen, or heard, any news lately. They even immobilised the car radio. Could you . . . ?'

'Yes,' M leaned back. 'At least we've now got a small idea of what it's about. We know where, and how. What? Well, that's a very different matter.'

'Sir,' Bond prompted.

'It's been kept under wraps for some time – a good few months in fact,' M began. 'These things always take the devil of a time to organise, and the participants wanted it to remain very low profile. Tonight, members of a Summit Conference are to arrive in Geneva. In fact, the first main session *is* this very night. They've taken over the whole of Le Richemond Hotel for three days . . .'

'Who, sir?'

'Russia, the United States, Britain, France and West Germany. The President of the United States, the French President, the Chairman of the USSR, the German Chancellor, and our Prime Minister – with all advisers, secretaries, military, the entire circus. The discussions will be on arms control and a more positive and prosperous future. The usual pie-in-the-sky.'

'The airship?' Bond's heart was sinking. The more he heard, the less he liked it.

'Goodyear. They have their ship, *Europa*, in Switzerland at the moment. When they heard about the Summit, Goodyear asked permission to fly what they called a goodwill mission, taking them straight over Le Richemond. They've got the *Europa* tethered just up the lake on a small strip – a tiny satellite field you can approach only from the lake itself. Mountain rescue boys and some private flyers use it.'

'But when did Goodyear arrange this?' Bond had not heard a whisper about any Summit Conference.

M grunted. 'You know what it's like, 007. They arrange their flights a year in advance. The *Europa* would have been there in any case. Would have been flying. However, they had to get permission once the Conference was announced.'

Percy had caught on. 'Dr Amadeus, when did you first hear about the Balloon Game?'

About four months ago, he told her, four or five.

'And the Summit . . . ?'

'It's been pencilled in for almost a year,' said M. 'The information was available only through diplomatic channels. The Press have been good boys for a change. Not a whisper, even though they must have known.'

Bill Tanner returned with the news that he had been in contact with Geneva.

'I talked to the Goodyear security man out at the strip. No problems, and we've alerted the Swiss police. They're going to close the field to everyone but accredited Goodyear staff. That means around thirty to thirty-five people, handlers, publicity and PR, mechanics, two pilots. Nobody's going to get in unless the Goodyear representatives okay the bona fides. It's sewn up, sir.'

'Right. Well, 007, all we have to do now is sew up the remainder of this unpleasant lot. Any ideas?'

Bond had one idea, and one only.

'You give me the EPOC frequency, sir – the real one, just in case they already have it, because I wouldn't put anything past SPECTRE and this crowd who are doing their dirty work for them.'

'Oh yes, the EPOC frequency. That was mentioned in your message. Made us think. Tell me about that, 007.'

Bond went through the essentials of the story, from start to finish, leaving out nothing.

'They claimed to have the Russian equivalent, sir, and the

emergency ciphers for both Russia and the USA. I'm inclined to believe them.'

M nodded. 'Yes, SPECTRE's never been backward in acquiring information. Good job we've got the Goodyear field under wraps, Chief-of-Staff. Chivvy the Swiss, would you, and keep in contact with the Goodyear people.'

M fiddled with his pipe as he began to expand on his own theory. If they did have the emergency ciphers of the United States and Russia, together with the frequencies, and if SPECTRE's agents were able to get near either of the leaders, they could activate that country's cipher.

'The way to do it,' Bond cut in, 'would be to hijack the airship and load enough shortwave hardware. Then take the *Europa* right over the very spot where heads of state are gathered together . . .'

'That's it, 007! Directly overhead would be enough for the United States' communications satellite to recognise the cipher, and, I presume, the Russian one as well.'

There were two possibilities: full nuclear strikes by one of the superpowers, or a simultaneous strike by both, knocking each of them out, leaving nothing but desolation on the two great continents for years to come. It was unthinkable. M said so, loudly. Bond pointed out that Jay Autem Holy had talked only of peace.

'There would be the danger of their using a reserve plan if I failed to return with the EPOC frequency.'

'There's one alternative. Ploughshare.' M said it as though this were the answer to everyone's dreams. 'Ploughshare, and whatever the Russian equivalent is.'

Percy asked what Ploughshare was, and M told her with a smile that it was a way of consigning all nuclear weapons – the bulk of them anyway – to the scrap heap. Quietly he informed the assembly of the cipher which could be sent over the EPOC frequency that would set in motion the destruction of all arming codes, and the disarming of all nuclear weapons, strategic and tactical.

'It's been reckoned that the process would take around twenty-four hours in the USA. I should imagine it would be a little longer in the Soviet Union. Just as there's always been a Doomsday Machine, we've had a Swords to Ploughshare Machine for the last three decades.'

M pursed his lips and waited for this to sink in before continuing.

'It's there in case of some catastrophe, like a 67 per cent paralysis of the armed forces by nerve gas, or a genuine stalemate. Of course it's always been hoped that if the Ploughshare option were taken, it would be by mutual understanding. But it's there. And it's just as potentially dangerous as blowing two great nations to pieces, because using it would be the easiest way to destabilise the two superpowers, by removing their nuclear balance at a stroke. Do that, and the stage is set for real revolution, economic disaster and chaos.'

Bond was right. Let him be supplied with the EPOC frequency, and a homing device, one or two of the Armourer's more fancy pieces of equipment, and a good surveillance team. 'You can then go back from whence you came, 007. Somewhere along the way, they'll pick you up, and we'll track you – safe enough if the team stays well back.'

Without further ado the meeting broke up and they took Bond off into a side room, where Major Boothroyd wired three homing devices into his clothes, and one for luck into the heel of his right shoe. The Armourer then handed Bond a couple of small weapons, and they gave him five minutes with Percy.

She clung to him, kissed him and told him to take care. There would be time enough once this was over, Bond said, there was no doubt about it, and the haymaking season would last all summer. Percy smiled the knowing smile women the world over smile when they've got what they really want.

Back in the conference room, they gave him the EPOC

frequency that had come into effect at midnight. It was now one in the morning, and Bill Tanner gave the final hasty briefing.

'We've already got your homers on two scanners,' he said. 'Don't worry, James, they've a range of almost ten miles. The car behind will stay only a mile or so away. The one riding point is already on his way. We know the route, so as soon as you go astray, we'll be in action. One SAS team standing by. They'll be anywhere you want in a matter of minutes, in a straight line, as the chopper flies. Good luck.'

Even the centre of London was beginning to slow down. Bond had the Bentley on the Hammersmith Flyover, heading towards the M4, in less than twelve minutes. They had calculated that Holy and Rahani wouldn't try anything until he was well off the motorway.

It happened just after the Heathrow Airport turnoff.

First, a pair of cars, travelling very fast, forced the Bentley to give up the outside lane. Bond cursed them for a couple of fools and pulled into the middle lane. Before he realised what was happening the two cars reduced speed, riding beside him, keeping him in the centre, while two heavy goods lorries came up in the slow lane.

Bond increased speed, trying to slip away in the centre lane, but both cars and lorries were well tuned, and, too late, he realised the way ahead was blocked by a big, slow-moving refrigerated truck.

He braked and saw incredulously the rear doors open and a ramp slide out, its end riding on buffered wheels, fishtailing to the road surface, the whole contraption being driven with great precision.

The cars to the right and lorries on the left crowded him, like sheep dogs working together until he had no option left. With a slight jerk, the Bentley's front wheels touched the ramp. With the steering wheel bucking in his hands, Bond gave the engine a tweak and glided into the great white moving garage.

The doors clanged shut behind him. Lights came on, and the

door was opened. Simon stood beside the car, an Uzi tucked under one arm.

'Well done, James. Sorry we couldn't give you any warning. Now, there's not much time. Out of those clothes. We've brought the rest of your gear. Everything off, shoes as well, just in case they smelled a rat and bugged you.'

Hands grasped at his clothing, tearing it from him, handing over other things – socks, underwear, grey slacks, white shirt, tie, blazer, and soft leather moccasins.

When he turned round, Simon was behind him, now dressed in a chauffeur's uniform, and the van seemed to be slowing down and taking one of the exits. The ASP was handed back to him – a sign of good faith? He wondered if it was loaded.

The team had worked with such speed and proficiency that Bond hardly had time to take in what was going on. As the truck shuddered to a halt, Simon opened the Bentley's rear door, half pushing Bond into the back, and in a second the truck's doors were again open, and they were reversing out. Simon was in the driving seat.

'Well done, James. You got the frequency, I presume?' Jay Autem Holy said from beside him.

'Yes.' His voice sounded numb.

'I knew it. Good. Give it to me now.'

Bond parroted the figures, and the decimal point.

'Where are we going?'

Holy repeated the frequency, asking Bond for confirmation. By now they were moving smoothly back on to the motorway.

'Where are we going, James? Don't worry. We're going to live through an important moment in history. First, Heathrow Airport. All the formalities have been taken care of. As we're just a little late, we're cleared to drive straight up to our private jet. We're going to Switzerland. Be there in a couple of hours. Then we have another short journey. Then yet another kind of flight. I shall explain it all later. You see, yesterday morning, long before you woke for breakfast, while it was still dark, the team from

Erewhon carried out a very successful raid. They stole a small landing strip and an airship. In the morning, James, we're all going for an airship ride. To change history.'

A mile or so back down the road, the observer in the trail car had noted that their target seemed to pull off the motorway for a few minutes. 'We're closing on him. Can't make it out. You want me to call in?'

'Give it a couple of minutes.' The driver shifted in his seat.

'Ah. No.' The observer stared at the moving blip which was Bond's homer. 'No, it's okay. Looks as though they were right. He's still heading west. Lay you odds on them picking him up between Oxford and Banbury.'

But the Bentley had, in fact, just passed them, going in the opposite direction, hurling itself back towards Heathrow and a waiting executive jet.

18

THE MAGIC CARPET

The executive jet had Goodyear symbols all over it – a smart livery, with the words *Good Year* flanking the winged sandal. It also had a British registration.

Bond resisted the temptation to make a run for it, try to attract attention, or cause a commotion. The realisation that he was outnumbered, outgunned and at an extreme disadvantage held him back. Whoever had laid out the ground plan of this operation, Holy, Rahani, or the inner council of SPECTRE itself, had done so with admirable attention to detail. For all he knew, the whole gang on board could have a genuine affiliation to Goodyear. In any case, he did not even know whether the ASP was loaded. So far there was at least a small amount of trust between him and the main protagonists. Exploit that trust to the full, he told himself, and just go along for the ride.

After takeoff, an attractive girl served drinks and coffee. Bond took the coffee, not wishing to dull any of his senses. He then excused himself and went to the pocket-sized lavatory at the rear of the aircraft.

The ever-watchful Simon sat near the door, eyeing him with wary amusement. But there was no attempt at restraint.

Inside he took out the ASP and slipped the magazine from the butt. It was, as he had thought, empty. Whatever else happened, ammunition or another weapon was a priority.

Back in his seat, Bond took stock. The takeover of the Goodyear base, together with the airship *Europa*, had already taken place hours before Bill Tanner had checked. True, the Swiss police were now alerted, but they would only make SPECTRE's task easier by keeping out any unwanted meddlers. The only possibility of the Service suspecting anything amiss would be the discovery that the surveillance cars had lost him – but heaven knew when they would find out. These people had taken no chances. By stripping him, they had effectively cut off any possible pursuit. The surveillance teams could be led a pretty dance, all over the country, following the constant bleeps of the homers coming from a pile of clothes in a lorry or car.

Not for the first time in his career, Bond was truly alone, with no way of warning anyone in authority. On the face of it, there was very little he could do to stop the airship's scheduled flight over Geneva, or prevent use of the Russian and American ciphers. Even the high-security classification of these ciphers would work against them. If M was correct and the SPECTRE plan turned on the operation of the American Ploughshare cipher or its Russian equivalent, there would be no worldwide alert while Russian and American leaders were locked in their Summit talks. The damage would already have been done before they knew there was a crisis.

Sitting next to Jay Autem Holy, he reflected on the ingenuity of the plan, which would denude the two superpowers of their one true weapon in the power balance. It was, of course, what many people had dreamed of, protested for, talked and argued about for years. M had stressed this at the meeting in the house off Northumberland Avenue. He was convinced that a phased run-down of both sides' nuclear armouries was a reasonable solution. For the two superpowers to be stripped overnight of their major weapons would destroy the tenuous stability that had prevailed since the Second World War. Operation Down Escalator was, Bond thought, an appropriate name, borrowing from that clumsy term, de-escalation, bandied about by politicians and protesters alike.

He dozed, not asleep, but conserving his energies for the time when ingenuity and strength might be needed. Yet in that state, pictures of the aftermath of Down Escalator, as described by his chief, churned over and over in his mind. There would be a worldwide economic crisis, with a market crash of enormous proportions, all confidence lost in the two superpowers. M had said that any economist or social historian could map out the events which would follow the undercutting of financial stability. The United States and the Soviet Union would be at the mercy of any other nation, however small, which possessed its own nuclear capability. As he took in the pictures M had drawn, Bond became even more determined to prevent Operation Down Escalator, no matter what the cost to himself. 'Anarchy will rule,' M had said. 'The world will divide into uncertain alliances and the man in the street, no matter what his birthright, nationality, or politics, will be forced to accept a way of life which will drop him into a dark and bitter well of misery. Freedom, even the compromise freedom which exists now, will be erased from our existence,' M had declaimed in a rare burst of almost Churchillian oratory.

'Seatbelt, James.' He opened his eyes. Jay Autem Holy was shaking his shoulder. 'We're coming in to land.'

Bond smiled back, sheepishly, as though he had really been deeply asleep.

'Landing? Where?'

Perhaps in Geneva, at the airport, he could get away, raise the alarm.

'Berne, Switzerland. You remember we're flying into Switzerland?'

Of course. They wouldn't do anything like trying to go into Geneva, which would be bristling with security. Berne! Bond smiled inwardly. These people had the whole business tied up. Berne, cars, a swift drive over to the Lake of Geneva and the Goodyear airstrip. All formalities would be already dealt with under the auspices of the huge international company they appeared to represent.

He glanced at his watch. It was already four in the morning. As the aircraft banked on its final approach he saw out of the cabin window that the sky was beginning to brighten, a dark grey colourwash streaked with light.

No, he had to go all the way. Try to spike the plan from the inside as it got under way.

'Nice place, Berne,' he observed casually, and Holy nodded.

'We go on by car. It'll take us an hour – an hour and a half. There'll be plenty of time. Our job does not start until eleven.'

They came in with engines throttled back, then there was a final short burst of power to lift them over the threshold, and hardly a bump as the wheels touched down, before the final fiery roar of reverse thrust.

As he had suspected, the transfer was swift and accomplished with the combined efficiency of Swiss bureaucracy and SPECTRE's cunning. The aircraft was parked well away from the main terminal. Two Audi Quattros and a police car were drawn up alongside.

From the window, Bond saw the transaction take place – the small pile of passports handed over, inspected and returned, with a salute. There would be no customs inspection, he thought. The Goodyear jet must have been running in and out of Berne and Geneva for a month or so now. They would have the formalities cut down to the fine art of mutual trust.

Then General Zwingli eased his bulk down the aisle first, giving Bond a friendly nod as he passed. They left the aircraft in single file, with Bond hemmed in neatly by the Arab boy and Simon. Nobody threatened him, but it was implicit in their looks that any false move would be countered. The police car, with its immigration officers on board, was already slowly disappearing back towards the terminal.

The Audis had Goodyear VIP stickers on the windscreens and rear windows. Bond recognised both drivers, in their grey uniforms, as men he had seen in Erewhon.

Within minutes, he was sitting next to Holy in the rear of the second car as they swept away from the airport in the half light of dawn. The houses on Berne's outskirts still slept, while others appeared to be just waking – lights coming on, green shutters open. Always, in Switzerland, Bond thought, you knew you were in a small, rich country, for all the buildings looked as though they had been assembled in some sterile room from a plastic kit, complete with small details of greenery and flowers.

They took the most direct route – straight to Lausanne, then along the lake road, following the line of the toy-like railway. Holy was quiet for most of the journey, but Simon, sitting in the front passenger seat, occasionally turned back to make small talk.

'You know this part of the world, James? Fairytale country, isn't it?'

Bond remembered, for no apparent reason, that the first time he had visited the Lake of Geneva was when he was sixteen. He had spent a week with friends in Montreux, had had a youthful holiday affair with a waitress from a lakeside café, and had developed a taste for Campari-soda.

Between Lausanne and Morges the cars stopped at a lighted lakeside restaurant. Simon and the Arab boy, in turns, brought out coffee and rolls to the cars. The sheer normality of their actions grated on Bond's nerves, like a probe on a raw tooth. Half of his mind and body urged him to take drastic action now: the other more professional half told him to wait; bide his time and use the moment when it came.

'Where are we heading?' he asked Holy soon after the breakfast break.

'A few kilometres this side of Geneva.' Holy remained relaxed and confident. 'We turn off the lake road. There's a small valley and an airstrip. The team from Erewhon will be waiting for us. Have you ever flown in an airship, James?'

'No.'

'Then it will be a new experience for us both. I'm told it's rather fantastic.' He peered from the windows. 'And it looks as though we'll have a clear day for it. The view should be wonderful.'

They went through Nyon, the houses clustered together on the lake as though clinging to each other to save themselves from falling in. Soon afterwards, Geneva came into view at the western end of the lake, a misty blur of buildings with a toy steamer ploughing a lone furrow of spray, chugging across the water. It all looked as peaceful as ever.

They also met the first police checkpoint, the cars slowing almost to a standstill before the sharp-eyed uniformed men waved them on.

There was a second road block just before they turned inland. A car and two policemen on motorcycles started to flag them down, until they spotted the Goodyear stickers. They were waved on with smiles. As Bond looked back, he saw one of the men talking into a radio. As he had imagined, the police were assisting innocently in the events planned to take place over the lake in a few hours' time.

The great cleft in the mountains seemed to widen as they climbed away. The sun was up now, and you could clearly see tiny farmhouses on the slopes. Then suddenly the valley floor and the tiny landing strip appeared just below them, the grass a painted green, the control tower, hangar and one other building as neat and unreal as a film set. Out on the grass, two mountain rescue aircraft stood like stranded birds. At the far end of the field the sausage shape of the Goodyear airship *Europa* swung lazily, tethered to her low portable masthead.

Then the road dipped, the airfield disappeared, and they were twisting through the S-bends which would carry them to the final destination.

Before the two cars reached the valley floor and the airstrip two more police checkpoints were negotiated. The Swiss police had certainly snapped into action. London, Bond decided, would feel very satisfied, content that nothing untoward could now happen by the peaceful lakeside.

There were no less than three police cars at the airstrip entrance, which was little more than a metal gateway set into an eight-foot chain-link fence, encircling the entire area. In the distance, a police car patrolled the perimeter slowly and as thoroughly as only the Swiss perform their official duties.

As the Audis drew up, Bond saw two more faces which he recognised from Erewhon. This time, though, the men were dressed in smart suits and smiled broad, almost ingratiating smiles as the two-vehicle convoy came to a halt. They exchanged a few words with the senior policeman on the gate, and the cars were waved forward. One man got into each car.

The man who entered Holy's car was a German, fair-haired, suspicious, and with features cut from a solid block of rough stone. He appeared to be in his mid-twenties, and the smart suit bulged around the breast pocket. Bond did not like the look of him. He liked him even less when the talking started.

Holy confined himself to the most pertinent questions, and was given precise, military answers in an American accent.

Posing as the Goodyear head of PR, Rudi, the German, had taken the call from Bill Tanner, which he now described in detail, saying the man was certainly English, and also undoubtedly represented one of the major British security agencies. The police, he said, began to arrive within half an hour of his call.

Jay Autem then asked about times, and you could tell from his expression he had already worked out that the enquiries had begun while Bond was in the Foreign Office house off Northumberland Avenue.

'James, you didn't say anything indiscreet when you were with your friend Anthony Denton?'

The two cars were heading not for the little office building but for the hangar, with its two slab-winged observation-rescue Pilatus aircraft sitting outside.

'Me?' Bond looked surprised and startled, as though he had not been paying attention to the conversation. 'Indiscreet? How? Why?'

Holy looked at him, a shadow of concern crossing his face.

'You see, James, Tamil's people took over this airstrip, and the whole organisation here, in the early hours of yesterday morning. Nobody suspected, there was no trouble. Not until last night, when you were closeted with the DSOFO, obtaining the EPOC frequency for us. Why, I ask myself, should the authorities begin to take an interest at that time of night?'

Bond shrugged, indicating that he had no idea, and, in any case, it was nothing to do with him.

The cars came to a halt. 'I do hope you've given us the correct frequency, James. If you haven't . . . Well, I've already warned you of the consequences; consequences for the entire world, my friend . . .'

'That's the current EPOC frequency. Have no doubt, Dr Holy,' he snapped back.

Holy winced at the sound of his real name, then nodded as he leaned forward to open the door.

Bond was left with the Arab boy, who watched him with alert bright eyes, a small Walther automatic clutched in his right hand. The safety catch, Bond noticed, was off.

Simon, Holy and the German, Rudi, were joined by Rahani and General Zwingli – a little procession walking spryly towards the hangar. Rahani's men were everywhere, Bond now saw, spread out, half concealed by what cover they could find, with a full armament of carbines and automatic weapons. There were even two guards on the small door inserted in one of the great sliding doors of the hangar.

The door was opened, and the party stepped inside. Two minutes later, Simon came out, walking quickly to the car.

'Colonel Rahani wants you inside.'

His manner was one of indifference, the attitude of a man who does not wish to become involved with anyone outside his own tight comradeship. Bond recognised the psychology. He had studied the whole subject of terrorist mentality and he knew they had come to some cut-off point. Simon was not willing to have any kind of relationship with Bond now. It could be, he thought, as they walked the few paces towards the hangar, that this really is the end. They've decided I've talked, and there can be no trust from now on. Curtain time – the fiction meeting the reality.

The little group of senior men stood just inside the door, and it was Tamil Rahani who greeted him.

'Ah, Commander Bond. We thought you should see this.' He gestured towards the centre of the hangar.

About forty men sat close together on the floor, held in a tight knot by three tripod-mounted machine guns trained on them, each with a crew of four.

'These are the good men from Goodyear.' He split the Goodyear, as though trying a pun. 'They will remain here until our mission is completed. They will be quickly dispatched – all of them – if one person makes an attempt to break out. They are being fed and looked after by the other team.' He indicated four men placed between the guns. 'It is uncomfortable for them. But if all goes well, they will be released unharmed. You will notice there is one lady.'

From the middle of the group, Cindy Chalmer gave Bond a wan smile, and Tamil Rahani lowered his voice. 'Between ourselves, Commander Bond, I think the delightful Miss Chalmer does not have much chance of surviving. But we want no bloodshed yet; not even your blood. You see, it was SPECTRE's intention that you should be put with this group of prisoners once you'd fulfilled your mission. The representative from SPECTRE did not trust you from the start, and is not at all happy with you now. However . . .' His lips drew back, not into a smile, but rather in a straight thin slash across his face. 'However, I think you can be of use in the airship. You can fly, can't you? You have a pilot's licence?'

Bond nodded, adding that he had no experience of airships.

'You'll only be the co-pilot. The one who sees to it that the pilot does as he's told. There'll be a nice irony in it, if by any chance you *have* doubled on us, Commander Bond. Come!'

They returned to the cars and drove swiftly over the few hundred yards to the office building. Inside, around forty of Rahani's trained men from Erewhon were sitting around, smoking and drinking coffee.

'Our handling team, Commander Bond. They have learned by simulation. At Erewhon. It was something we did not show you, but they are very necessary when we weigh out the airship before takeoff – and, to a great extent, when we get back from our short excursion.'

The only man who was out of place sat at a table just inside the door. He wore a navy blue pilot's uniform, and his peaked cap lay on the table in front of him. One of Rahani's men sat opposite, well clear of the table, with an Uzi machine pistol ready to blow the man's stomach out should he make a fuss.

'You are our pilot, I presume?' Rahani smiled politely at the man, who looked at him coldly and said he was a pilot, but he would not fly under duress.

'I think you will,' Rahani said confidently. 'What do we call you?'

'You call me Captain,' the pilot replied.

'No. We're all friends here. Informal.' Rahani added in a commanding snap: 'Your first name.'

The pilot realised it would be foolhardy to remain too stubborn. He cocked his head on one side.

'Okay, you can call me Nick.'

'Right, Nick . . .' Tamil Rahani carefully explained what was going to happen. Nick was to fly the airship, just as he would have done under normal circumstances. Up to Geneva and along the lake front. After that he would change course, cutting straight over Le Richemond Hotel – 'Where the Summit Conference is in progress. You will stay over the hotel for approximately four minutes.' Rahani spoke like an officer used to being obeyed. 'Four minutes at the outside. No more. Nothing will happen. Nobody will be hurt as long as you do what you're told. After that, you will bring the airship back here and land. You may then leave unharmed.'

'Damned if I will.'

'I think you will, Nick. Someone else will do it if you don't. This gentleman here, for instance.' He touched Bond's shoulder. 'He's a pilot, without airship experience, but he will do it if we give him enough encouragement. Our encouragement to you is that we kill you straight away, here and now, if you don't agree.'

'He means it, Nick,' Bond interrupted. 'In a couple of minutes you'll just be a lump of meat. Useless to anyone. Best do as he says.'

The pilot thought for a moment, recognising his inescapable position.

'Okay. Okay, I'll fly the blimp.'

'Good, Nick. And thank you, Commander Bond.' Rahani went on in a level voice, 'Now I'll tell you what we have in store for Commander Bond. He is to be your co-pilot. You will tell him now about the differences between flying an aircraft and handling an airship. We shall give him one round of ammunition for his automatic pistol. One round only. He can wound or kill only one person with that, and there'll be five of us on board; five, not counting Commander Bond and yourself. Bond here will do exactly as I tell him. If you try to be clever, I shall tell him to kill you. If he does not kill you, one of us will do it for him, and force him to take over. If he still resists, then we'll kill him too, and manage the best we can. I understand that this airship is filled with helium and ballasted so that it will stay up, unassisted, for some time, and is difficult to crash. Yes?'

'Guess you're right.'

'Well, Commander Bond will look after you, and we'll all have a pleasant trip. How long will it take? Half an hour?'

'About that. Maybe three-quarters.'

'Commander Bond, talk to your pilot. Learn from him. We

have things to get on board the gondola.' He gave Bond a hard knock on the shoulder. 'Learn, and do as you are bidden, eh?'

Bond lowered his head as he sat down, letting it come near the pilot's, his lips hardly moving. 'I'm working under some duress as well. Just help me. We have to stop them.' Then he said aloud, 'Okay Nick, just tell me about this ship.'

The pilot looked up, puzzled for a moment, but Bond nodded encouragement, and he began to talk.

Around them, Rahani's men were carrying equipment out of the office. Among the hardware was one powerful shortwave transmitter and a micro. Bond listened attentively as Nick told him that flying the airship was more or less the same as handling an aircraft.

'Yoke, rudder pedals, same flight instruments, throttles for the two little engines. The only difference is in trimming.' He explained how the two small balloons, fore and aft in the helium-filled envelope, could be inflated with air, or have the air valved off. 'It's more or less the same principle as a balloon, except, with the air-filled ballonets, you don't have to bleed off expensive gas. You just take on or dump air. The ballonets take care of the gas pressure, give you extra lift, or allow you to trim up or down. The only tricky bit is knowing when to dump the pressure as you come in to land, positioning the blimp, so that the ground crew can grab at the guy ropes. You need to bleed it all off at that point, like dumping ballast, so nobody gets lifted off the ground.'

It was all technically straightforward, and Nick even made a little drawing to show Bond where the valves lay, above the forward windshield, and how the ballonets were filled with air from scoops below the small engines. He had hardly finished when Simon came over, glancing at his watch. They looked up, to find the office almost deserted.

'You're both needed at the ship.' He held up one round of 9mm ammunition, and Bond saw that it was one of his original Glaser slugs. 'You get this when we're aboard.' His eyes showed no sympathy. 'Come along, then. We've got to show the flag. One joy ride around the lake.'

Over at the airship, Rahani's men had prepared themselves to take up the strain on the forward guy ropes hanging from the great pointed sausage of the airship, which at the moment remained tethered to its mooring mast.

As they reached the ship, they could see the others were already on board the curved gondola, which seemed to hang under the great gleaming envelope.

Nick climbed up first through the large door which took up a third of the gondola's right-hand side. Bond followed, with Simon taking up the rear and pulling the door closed behind him.

Tamil Rahani sat next to Holy at the back of the gondola. In front of them they had arranged the transmitters linked to the computer. The Arab boy sat directly in front of Holy, with General Zwingli across the narrow aisle from him. Bond went forward, taking his place on Nick's right. Simon now hovered between them.

As soon as he was in his seat, Nick became the complete professional, showing Bond the instrumentation, and pointing out the all-important valves for the ballonets.

'Whenever you're ready,' Rahani called out, but Nick did not answer. He was busy with the pre-flight checks, sliding his window open to shout down to the man in command of the ground crew.

'Okay,' he called. 'Tell your boys to stand by. I'm starting up, and I'll give you a thumbs-up when they have to take strain.' To Bond, he said he would be starting the port engine first, and immediately afterwards the starboard would fire. 'We fill the ballonets straight away, and as they're filling I shall release us from the mooring mast. The chaps outside, if they've been trained correctly, will take the strain and dump the ballast hanging from the gondola. After that, I trim the ship, lift the nose and,' he turned, grinning, 'we'll see if they have the sense to let go of the guy ropes.'

Reaching forward, Nick started both engines, one after the other, very fast, and set the air valves to fill. As Bond watched, Simon leaned forward, felt inside his jacket and removed the ASP. There was a double click as one round went into the breech, then the weapon was handed back. 'You kill him, if the Colonel gives the order. If you try anything clever, I'll shoot you.'

Bond did not even acknowledge him. By now he was following everything that Nick was doing, opening the throttles, pulling the lever that moored them to the mast, monitoring the pressure.

The airship's nose tilted upwards, and Nick waved to the ground crew as he gave the engines full throttle. The nose slid higher and there was a tiny sensation of buoyancy, then, very slowly they moved forwards and upwards – rock-steady, no tremor or vibration as they climbed away from the field. It was like riding on a magic carpet.

19

PLOUGHSHARE

In his time James Bond had either flown, or flown in, most types of aircraft, from the old Tiger Moth biplane to Phantom jets. Yet never had he experienced anything like the *Europa*.

The morning was clear and sunny. With its two little engines humming like a swarm of hornets, its single-blade wooden airscrews blurring into twin discs, the fat silver ship glided out from the wide cleft in the mountains, over the road and railway lines, and climbed above the lake. It would have been an enchanted moment for anyone, like Bond, who loved machines. At a thousand feet, gazing out at the spectacular view of lake and mountains he even forgot for a few seconds the horrifying and dangerous mission they were embarked upon.

It was the stability of the ship that amazed him most. There was a complete lack of any buffeting experienced at that height and over that type of terrain in a conventional aircraft. No wonder those who travelled on the great airships of the 1920s and 1930s fell in love with them.

The *Europa* dipped its nose, almost stood on it, turning a full circle. At fifteen hundred feet they had a panoramic view of the lake: the mountain peaks touched with snow against the light blue sky, Montreux in the distance, the French side of the lake with the town of Thonon looking peaceful and inviting.

Then Nick eased the ship around so that they could see Geneva as they approached at a stately fifty miles per hour.

Bond turned his head to look at the rear of the gondola.

Rahani and Jay Autem Holy ignored the view, hunched over the transmitter. They had folded down some of the seat backs, so that Bond had a good view of the radio, seeing that it was linked to the micro.

Holy appeared to be muttering to himself as he tuned to the frequency. Rahani watched him closely, like a warder, Bond thought. General Zwingli was half-turned in his seat, giving advice. Both Simon and the Arab boy stood guard, the boy never taking his eyes off the pilot and Bond. Simon was leaning against the door, almost as though he were covering his masters.

Below them, the lakeside of Geneva slid into view. The airship slowed, tilted forward and turned gently.

'No playing around, Nick,' Rahani called in warning. 'Just do what you normally do. Then take her straight over Le Richemond.'

'I'm doing what I normally do. I'm doing it by the book,' the pilot said laconically. 'That's what you wanted and that is just what you're getting.'

'And what,' Bond called back, '*are* we really doing, anyway? What is this caper that's going to change history?'

Holy lifted his eyes towards the flight deck.

'We are about to put the stability of the world's two most powerful nations to the test. Would you believe that the ciphers directly transmittable to the emergency networks of the American President and the Chairman of the USSR include programs to deactivate their main nuclear capabilities?'

'I'd believe anything.' Bond did not need to hear any more. M was right. The intention was to send the US Ploughshare program, and its Russian counterpart, into their respective satellites, and from there into irreversible action. It was at this moment that Bond made up his mind.

His whole adult life had been dedicated to his country; this time he knew it would be forfeit. There was one Glaser slug in the ASP. With luck, in the confined gondola it would blow any one of the men in half. But only one. So what was the use of a human target? Kill one, then be killed. That would serve no purpose. If he chose the right time, and the Arab boy could be distracted, the one Glaser slug, placed accurately, would blow the radio and possibly the micro as well.

He would die very soon after taking out the hardware, but for Bond this was as nothing compared to the satisfaction of knowing he would once more have smashed SPECTRE's plans. Maybe they would try again. But there were always other men like himself, and the Service had been alerted.

Geneva, clean, ordered and picturesque, now lay to their right, as Nick gently turned the ship. Mont Blanc towered above them. The airship began to descend to a thousand feet for its short journey along the lakeside.

'How long?' It was the first time Zwingli had spoken to the men at the controls.

Nick glanced back. 'To Le Richemond? About four minutes.'

'Are you locked onto that frequency?' The General was now addressing Holy.

'We're on the frequency, Joe. I've put the disk in. All we have to do is press the Enter key, and we shall know whether comrade Bond has been true to his word.'

'You're activating the States first, then?'

'Yes, Joe.' Rahani replied this time. 'Yes, the United States get their instructions in a couple of minutes.' He craned forward to look from the window. 'There it is, coming up now.'

Bond gently slid the safety catch off the ASP.

'Ready, Jay. Any minute.' Rahani did not raise his voice, yet the words carried clearly over the length of the gondola.

The luxurious hotel with its perfectly laid out gardens was coming up below them. Nick held the *Europa* on a true course which would take them straight over the palatial building.

'I said ready, Jay.'

'Any second . . . Okay,' Holy answered.

At that moment, Bond, gripping the ASP, turned towards the Arab boy and shouted, 'Your window. Look to your window.'

The Arab turned his head slightly, and Bond, knowing there was one chance, and one chance only, brought his hand up and squeezed the trigger. In the whirling engine noise, the solid clunk of the pistol's firing mechanism crashing forward obliterated everything.

For a second he could not believe it. Was it a misfire? A dud round? Then came Simon's laugh, echoed by a grunt from the Arab boy.

'Don't think of throwing it, James. I'll cut you down with one hand. You didn't honestly think we'd let you on board with a loaded gun, did you? Too much of a risk.'

'Damn you, Bond.' Rahani was half out of his seat. 'No gunplay – not in here. Have you given us the frequency, or is that as false as your own loyalty?'

The bleep and whir from the back of the gondola indicated that Holy had activated the cipher program. He gave a whoop of joy.

'It's okay, Tamil. Whatever else Bond's tried, he *has* given us the frequency. The satellite's accepted it.'

Bond dropped the pistol, a useless piece of metal. They had done it. At this moment, the sophisticated hardware in the Pentagon would be sorting the digits at the unbelievable rate of today's computers. The instructions would be pouring out to compatible machines the length and breadth of the USA and to the NATO forces in Europe. Now it was done, Bond felt only a terrible anger and a sickness deep in his stomach.

What happened in the next few seconds took time to sink in. Holy was still whooping his joy as he half rose, stretching out a hand, fingers snapping, towards Rahani. 'Tamil, come on, the Russian program. You have it. I've locked on to their frequency . . .' His voice rose with urgency. 'Tamil!' Now shouting, 'Tamil! The Russian program. Quickly.'

Rahani gave a great bellowing laugh. 'Come on, yourself, Jay. You didn't think we were really going to allow the Soviet Union to suffer the indignity of being stripped of her assets as well?'

Jay Autem Holy's mouth opened and closed, like a dying fish. 'Wha . . . ? Wha . . . ? What do you mean, Tamil? What . . . ?'

'Watch them!' Rahani snapped, and both Simon and the Arab boy appeared to stiffen to his command. 'You can begin the return journey, Nick,' Rahani said, so quietly that Bond was amazed he could be heard above the steady motor buzz.

'I mean, Jay, that long ago I took over as the Chief Executive of SPECTRE. I mean that we have done what we set out to do. I even gambled on the pawn, Bond, getting the EPOC frequency. Down Escalator was always intended simply to deal with the imperialist power of the United States, which we shall now be able to hand on a plate to our friends in the Soviet Union. You were brought in only to provide the training programs. We have no use for emotionally motivated fools like Zwingli and yourself. You understand me?'

Jay Autem Holy let out a wail of despair echoed only by General Zwingli's roar of anger.

'You bastard!' Zwingli started to move. 'I wanted my country strong again, by putting Russia and the USA on the same footing. You've sold out – you . . .' He launched himself at Rahani.

The Arab boy shot him, once, fast and accurately. He toppled over without a sound. While the blast of the boy's weapon continued in a long bell-like boom, echoing in the confined space, Jay Autem Holy leaped towards Rahani, arms outstretched to claw at his throat, his scream turning to a banshee wail of hate.

Rahani, with no room to back off, shot him in mid-leap, firing two rounds from a small hand gun. But Holy's powerful spring, strengthened by his fury, carried his body on so that he crashed lifeless on top of SPECTRE's leader, the man who had inherited the throne of the Blofeld family.

'Get us down,' Bond rapped at the pilot. 'Just get us down!' In the confusion, he made for the nearest target, Simon, who, with his back to the flight deck, was moving towards the tangle of bodies piled across the seats. Bond landed hard on Simon's back, one arm locking round his neck, the other delivering a mighty chopping blow which connected a fraction below the right ear.

Caught off balance, Simon fell to the left. His hand, scrabbling for some kind of hold, hit the gondola door's locking device so that the door swung open, bringing in a sudden draught of air. As Simon went limp, the Arab boy fired at Bond, a fraction of a second late, for the bullet hit Simon's chest. At the moment of his death, a great power seemed to force itself through his muscles, so that he broke free from Bond's grasp, the body turning as it crumpled, the reflexes closing his hand around the grip and trigger of the Uzi machine pistol. Half a burst of fire rapped out, cutting the Arab almost in two.

Simon did not let go of the gun, but merely fell backwards. His hands did not claw air, no sound came from his throat. He simply fell through the gondola door, through a thousand feet of clear air, his last long journey to hit the water below.

Bond made to grab at the Arab's Walther, now lying on the floor. He felt the sting of a bullet cutting a shallow furrow along the flesh above his right hip and another sing past his ear.

He reached the Walther, but as he turned instinctively towards where Tamil Rahani should be, his finger on the trigger, he realised the instigator of this whole drama was not there.

'Parachute,' Nick said calmly. 'Little bastard had a parachute. Took the dive.'

Bond moved to the gondola door and, hanging on to the grab rail, leaned out.

Below, against the blue-grey water of the lake, was the white shape of Rahani's parachute, a light breeze carrying him away from Geneva, towards the French side of the lake.

'They're bound to pick him up,' Bond said aloud.

'Could you close the door, please.' Nick's voice was as calm as only an experienced pilot's can sound under stress. 'I've got to find somewhere to drop this blimp.'

He switched on the flight radio, flicking the dial with finger and thumb, adjusting the headset he had not been allowed to wear throughout the flight. A few seconds later, he turned his head slightly as Bond slumped into the seat beside him.

'We can go back to the strip. Apparently the Swiss military cleared it soon after we left. Looks as if we've had guardian angels watching over us.'

They sat together on the balcony of a private room in the lakeside hotel: M, Bill Tanner, Cindy Chalmer, Percy and Bond, whose side still stung from the long bullet burn, although it was now dressed.

'You mean,' Bond said with cold anger, 'that you already knew they had taken over the airstrip? You knew when you sent me off from London?'

M nodded. He had told Bond how, because of the tight security surrounding the Summit Conference, anyone who was authorised had been given identifying ciphers.

On the night Bond had visited the house, off Northumberland Avenue, Bill Tanner's call to the Goodyear people had not elicited the correct sequence.

'We knew something had gone wrong,' said M calmly. 'We alerted everyone with need-to-know, arranged with the United States and the Soviet Union that any messages on their current emergency satellite frequencies should be accepted, but not passed on. Just a precaution. I mean, you can always be trusted, 007.'

'Thank you,' Bond said with icy calm.

'Now look, 007,' M said sharply. 'It's no good running away with the idea you're indispensable.'

'I was to be thrown to the wolves then,' Bond almost shouted. 'It wasn't necessary to leave me in outer darkness, as you once so neatly put it, but you let me go, knowing full well . . .'

'Come, come. How dare you reproach your superiors in this way,' M put in tartly. Suddenly he leaned forward and placed a hand gently on Bond's arm and said in an uncharacteristic tone of paternal concern, 'It was for your own good as much as ours,

James. After all, you might have found a way of bringing in Holy – or Rahani, come to that. But that wasn't uppermost in our minds. We had to find a way of restoring your good name. Look on it as a sort of rehabilitation.'

'Rehabilitation?' Bond spat the word out with scorn.

'You see,' M went on quietly, 'there had to be some role you could play for the sake of your public image. The Press could hardly fail to notice high jinks on an airship directly over the place where the Summit talks were going on. Geneva's been stiff with journalists these past few days. We told the Swiss authorities they could let a certain amount of reporting through. Saves us a tricky hushing-up job in a way. I think you'll be pleased with what the papers say tomorrow. Might not be a bad idea to get another question tabled in the House.'

Bond was silent. He gazed at M, who gave his arm a couple of reassuring pats before withdrawing his hand.

'I suppose you'll want to take some sick leave because of that scratch,' M said distantly.

Bond and Percy exchanged looks. 'If it wouldn't inconvenience the Service, sir.'

'A month, then? Let all this fuss die down. We can't have the whole Department going public for the sake of your honour, 007.'

Cindy spoke for the first time. 'What about Dazzle? Mrs St John-Finnes?'

Tanner told them there had been no trace of the lady who called herself Dazzle; just as Rahani had disappeared into thin air. A launch picked up his 'chute. He had drifted well inshore, on the French side.

'Damn. I wanted a little time alone with that bastard.' The delightful Cindy Chalmer could be lethal when roused.

Percy gave her a wicked smile. 'You, Cindy, are going straight back to Langley. The order came through this. morning.'

Cindy pouted, and Bond tried hard not to catch her eye. 'And what about Dr Amadeus?' he asked.

'Oh, we're taking care of him,' Bill Tanner said a little earnestly. 'We've always room for good computer men in the Service. Anyway, Dr Amadeus turned out to be a brave young man.'

'There *is* something else,' M grunted. 'The Chief-of-Staff did not know this but in checking back through the files when you alerted us to Rahani, 007, we found some interesting information. You recall we've been keeping surveillance on him for some time?'

Bond nodded as M slid a matt black and white print from the folder on his lap.

'Interesting?'

The photograph showed Tamil Rahani locked in an embrace with Dazzle St John-Finnes. 'Looks as though they had plans for the future.'

Bond asked about Erewhon and was told that the Israelis had pinpointed the site. 'Nobody there. Deserted. But they're keeping an eye on it. I doubt if Rahani will visit it again. But he'll probably show up somewhere.'

'Yes.' Bond's voice was flat. 'Yes, I don't think we've heard the last of him, sir. After all, he boasted that he was Blofeld's successor.'

'Come to think of it,' M mused, 'I wonder if you should forgo that leave, 007. It may be vital to follow up . . .'

'He's got to rest, sir, for a short time at least.' Percy was almost ordering M. This was something the Head of Service rarely experienced. He looked at the willowy ash-blonde, astonishment on his face.

'Yes. Yes. Well, if you put it like that . . . I suppose . . . Yes.'

20

END OF THE AFFAIR

They first flew to Rome, and stayed for a week at the Villa Medici. Percy had never been to Rome and Bond enjoyed showing her as much as one can fit into seven short days.

From Rome they travelled to Greece, to take an island-hopping tour, starting in the Aegean with a couple of nights on Naxos. They stayed only one night on Rhodes, because of the tourist hordes, and then doubled back, spending a night here, two nights there.

Another week took them to the Ionian sea, where they managed to find some secluded beaches and tavernas, off the package-holiday routes.

It was a time of distant voices from the past. The couple exchanged life-stories, told the long tales of their youth, made their separate confessions, and became totally immersed in each other's bodies. For Percy and Bond, the world became young again and time stood still, as only time can within the dark, secret mysteries of the Greek islands.

They ate lobster fresh from the sea and drank their fill of retsina. Sometimes the evenings ended with them dancing with the waiters under the vines of a roadside taverna, arm-stretching and calf-slapping. They discovered, as many have before, that the taverna-owners of the islands recognise the signs of love and take lovers to their hearts.

And during all their joy, Bond kept a wary eye on strangers, assuming that Percy, being a lady of the same trade, was doing likewise.

They did not spot the same face – or even the same jewellery, which can be more important – once. Vehicles, even motor-cycles, did not show up twice. They were free.

But SPECTRE's teams were numerous and clever. Neither James Bond nor Percy Proud could know of shadows creeping in around them.

The teams were usually five strong, and they changed daily, never using the same car twice, always having a tail ready to follow on to the next island. A girl in one place, a happy Greek boy in another; first a student, then a middle-aged English couple; old Volkswagens, brand-new Hondas, staid Peugeots. It was all the same to them. The leader's orders were clear, and when the right moment came, he too arrived.

Bond and Percy spoke much of the future, yet, in the last week, while heading for Corfu, from where they planned to fly to London direct, they still could not come to any decision even though they had talked of marriage.

As the trip drew to an end they found a small bungalow hotel, away from beehive modern glass and concrete palaces. It was close to a secluded beach, which could be reached only by clambering over rocks. Their room looked out on a slope of dusty olive trees and oddly Victorian-looking scrub.

Each day, in the late afternoon, they would return to their room, and, as dusk closed in and the cicadas began their endless song, the couple would make love, long and tender, with a rewarding fulfilment of a kind neither remembered experiencing before.

On their last night, with their packing to be done, and a special dinner ordered at the taverna, they followed their usual pattern, walking hand in hand up the slope from the beach, entering their room from the scrubby olive grove, and leaving the windows open and the blinds drawn.

They soon became lost in each other, murmuring the sweet

adolescent endearments, enjoying a private island of physical pleasure.

They were hardly aware of the darkness or the song of the night coming from the cicadas. Neither of them heard Tamil Rahani's car pull up quietly on the road below the hotel. Nor were they aware of his emissary, who moved, sure-footed in rope-soled sandals up from the road, treading softly through the olives until he reached the window.

Tamil Rahani, the successor to the Blofelds, had decreed they should both die, and he would be in at the death. His only regret was that it must be quick.

The short, sallow-faced man who was the most accomplished of SPECTRE's silent killers, peered through the lattice of the blinds, smiled and carefully withdrew a six-inch ivory blowpipe. With even greater care he loaded the tiny wax dart filled with deadly pure nicotine and began to slide the end of the pipe through the lattice. Percy lay, eyes closed, nearest the window.

Her reaction was conceived in long training, for she was like an animal in her instinct for danger. With a sudden move, she slid from under a startled Bond, one hand going for the floor and the small revolver that always lay at her side of the bed.

She fired twice, rolling naked on the floor as she did so – a textbook kill, the man clearly outlined through the blinds lifting back as though in slow motion, his dying breath expelling the wax dart into the air.

Bond was beside her in a second, the ASP in his hand. As they emerged into the night air, they heard the sound of Rahani's car on the road below the hotel. They needed no telling who it was.

Later, when the body had been removed, calls made to London and Washington, and police and other authorities were satisfied, Bond and Percy drove into Corfu Town itself, to spend the night in one of the larger hotels.

'Well, at least that settles it. We should both know now,' Percy began.

'Know?' They had managed to get a meal of sorts in their room, though Bond found it hard to relax.

'The future, James. We should both know about the future after that unpleasant episode.'

'You mean that until Blofeld's successor is dead, neither of us will have peace?'

'That's part of it. Not all, though.' She paused to sip her wine. 'I killed, James, automatically and . . .'

'And most efficiently, darling.'

'Yes, that's what I mean. We're not like other people, are we? We're trained, and tidied, and obey orders – fly into danger at a moment's notice.'

Bond thought for a moment. 'You're right, of course, darling. What you mean is that people like us can't just stop, or lead normal lives.'

'That's it, my dear James. It's been the best time. The very best. But . . .'

'But now it's over.'

She nodded, and he leaned across the table to kiss her. 'Who knows?' Bond asked of nobody in particular.

The next morning they rebooked tickets, and Bond saw her off, watching her aeroplane climb over the little hillock at the end of the runway, then turn to set course for Athens, where she would make her connection for Paris.

In an hour, he would be on his way back to London and one of his other lives, to play some other role for his country.